Informed
Consent

USA TODAY BESTSELLING AUTHOR
Melissa F. Miller

Brown Street Books

Copyright © 2015 Melissa F. Miller

Published by Brown Street Books.

For more information about the author,
please visit www.melissafmiller.com.

For more information about the publisher,
please visit www.brownstbooks.com.

Brown Street Books ISBN: 978-1-940759-12-8

Cover design by Clarissa Yeo

Book Layout & Design ©2015 - BookDesignTemplates.com

Dedicated to the talented members of the
Thomas E. Starzl Transplantation Institute's
Liver Transplantation Program at the
University of Pittsburgh Medical Center.

ACKNOWLEDGMENTS

As always, I owe a debt of thanks to both my family and my fantastic editing team.

1.

July
Boston, Massachusetts

D R. GRETA ALLSTROM KEPT HER hands in her lap to hide their trembling and tried to work up enough saliva in her dry mouth to answer the question Dexter Corgan had just asked. The three interchangeable, dark-suited, intense men seated around the table waited.

Corgan repeated the question. "How much do you need?"

She wet her lips. "To ramp up production and go to market within the next eighteen months?"

He bobbed his head in a curt nod. The motion drew attention to the prominent ridge in his brow. In the shadowy light of the basement bar, he resembled a Neanderthal man even more than he had in the light of day.

"Um, I'm a scientist, so the business end isn't my forte. Maybe forty million?" She had no earthly idea. But surely forty million dollars would produce a fleet of medical nano-robots.

The trio of suits laughed.

"That's pocket change, doctor. Think big," the one in the middle said.

"Eighty?" she croaked. It was a sum of money she couldn't even imagine. And she sensed it would come with unbreakable strings.

The middle one, who must have been the senior guy despite the fact that, like the others, he appeared to be in his late twenties, at most, spoke again. "Eighty is fine." He flicked his eyes toward Corgan. "Mr. Corgan didn't happen to explain the terms and conditions, did he?"

She shook her head no. Dexter Corgan had explained absolutely nothing. He'd raced up to her at a conference after she'd presented her paper on 'Theoretical Implications of Anti-Dementia Drug Delivery Through Nano-Robotic Means,' and pumped her hand with wild enthusiasm. He acted as if he were a fan gushing over a celebrity and not a venture capital consultant talking to a genetic researcher. Literally within thirty minutes, she'd found herself in this cramped underground Boston bar sitting next to Corgan and across the sticky surface of the scarred and scuffed wood table from three nameless would-be investors.

Just then Corgan stood. "I'm just the matchmaker," he told Greta. "These gentlemen retained me as a talent scout, you might say, and asked me to attend the conference, evaluate the presentations, and bring them the most promising idea." He paused and flashed her a smile. "And I have. Assuming you all reach an agreement, they'll pay me a finder's fee. But from this point forward, the negotiations are between you and them." He shook the proffered hands around the table, winked at Greta, and then hurried up the stairs and out of the bar.

It was as if he didn't want to hear what came next.

The middle guy pinned his eyes on hers. "We're a group of serious private investors, doctor, committed to helping cutting-edge ideas circumvent the federal funding morass and escape the constraints of the glacial pace of university research. We have the means and the will to help you make your innovation a reality."

She waited.

"Sounds too good to be true, doesn't it?" the man seated to his left said.

She turned her gaze to him and noticed that, unlike the others, his eyes were green. "It does."

"Right. Well, there are *some* hoops." He gave her a toothy smile. "One, the investment will be private, which means you don't report it to your Institutional Review Board Director."

"I can't ... that's not permitted," she protested.

"We know how to structure the deal so that it will work. That's *our* expertise. You focus on the science and let us handle the business," the middle guy said. "You'll tell your director that an investment group is going to fund the nano-robotics stage outside of the university structure. The university will license us the drug at that point."

"What if they don't want to?"

He laughed. "They will. We've done this before. We offer a very generous licensing fee. More money than your program receives from grants and donations in a year. And if the trials are successful, the university will continue to reap enormous royalties without taking the risks of development. Trust me, that's not a problem."

"But what about the current research? I have reporting requirements—"

"We'll partition it off. As far as the Department of Health and Human Services and the FDA are concerned, it'll be two separate studies—the drug study, which they'll oversee—and a privately funded robotics study. That's not your concern. You continue under the rules and regulations already in place for the drug study. We'll worry about the rest."

The guy on the left interjected. "Two, before we leave here, we'll agree on a timetable. Think carefully about how much time you need because there will be no extensions given."

"What if—?"

"None." His green eyes hardened into emerald marbles.

She swallowed and nodded, not trusting herself to speak.

"Three, if the project doesn't make it to market, we'll be looking to you to make us whole."

"I don't have eighty million dollars."

"Of course you don't. That's why you'll make sure the drug gets to market." He smiled.

She ignored the goosebumps that sprouted on her forearms. "But you wouldn't be able to collect. My guarantee would be worthless."

The men exchanged glances. After a moment, the man on the right, who up until then had been completely mute, spoke. "It's not a financial guarantee. It's a personal guarantee."

"I still don't understand."

The middle guy sighed. "This is tiresome. Instead of worrying about what happens if you fail, focus on succeeding, so you won't ever have to find out. But let's just say our organization will think of some work for you to do until the debt is repaid."

Visions of working in a meth lab in her underwear or performing cosmetic surgery on fugitives in a dim back alley flashed across her mind. "You know, I never caught your names," she blurted.

"You don't need to know our names. Our investment group is the Alpha Fund. That's all you need to know," the man on the left told her.

"What's the actual status of the drug trials?" the one in the middle asked.

"We're testing the supplement in live patients. So far, it's slowing their deterioration. It's very promising as is. But if we could deliver it to the myelin sheath directly, well, I'm convinced it will *stop* the deterioration in its tracks. It could be used as a preventative to avoid it entirely."

"What needs to happen before you test nano-robot delivery?"

"Well, the creation of the nano-robots, of course."

Green Eyes waved his hand at that. "We'll arrange that. What needs to happen with the drug trial?"

"I need to compare the gray matter of a control patient who exhibited no signs of dementia with brain slices from a dementia patient who received the drug and a patient whose dementia was uncontrolled."

"Just one of each? That's not very rigorous," the middle man observed.

"Given their ages and health issues, my research participants die fairly regularly. But many people are squeamish about post-mortem brain autopsies. They don't like to think about it. So I don't have a large pool of subjects who will consent. The numbers are limited by necessity but I have a robust computer model that will extrapolate from a small sample size. But obviously, the more samples the better," she hurried to explain.

"You understand that if we go forward we don't want to hear that you're behind schedule because nobody's died in a while," he pressed.

She stared at him. "That's out of my hands, though."

"Not if you take our money. If you take our money, you need to deliver. End of story."

Her heart raced and her shaking hands began to positively vibrate in her lap. She *needed* this funding. She *knew* the nano-robotic delivery would work. It would change lives. *She* would improve the quality of end of life for people all over the world. But these men, they scared her.

"What do you say, Dr. Allstrom?"

She couldn't hear the thumping music from the house band or the laughter of the revelers around her over the sound of her blood whooshing in her ears. She couldn't hear her own voice and didn't know if she whispered or shouted when she said, "I need some of my subjects to die."

2.

Late September
Portland, Maine

"I'M SO SORRY, Mr. Wynn," the doctor said, looking up from his chart and meeting Doug Wynn's hardened gaze with his own sad brown eyes. "You're running out of time. This last round of chemotherapy wasn't as successful as we'd hoped it would be. If you don't get a liver soon there's very little left that we can do."

Wynn nodded, set this mouth in a firm line, and looked past the doctor out the window, focusing on the cold, gray landscape.

"The transplant list, then?" he asked, dragging his eyes back to the man.

After several long moments of silence passed, the doctor began to fidget. He cleared his throat and shuffled through the papers on his clipboard. "No, I'm afraid that won't be an option. Your tumor size is too large. It disqualifies you from receiving a liver from a deceased donor."

"Just as well," Wynn said. He had a visceral, negative reaction to the thought of having the organ of a dead stranger placed in his body.

The doctor gave him a nonplussed look. Then he ventured, "Does that mean you've made some progress in locating your ... son, I believe it was? Your only real option now is a live donor."

Wynn took his time answering. "No, I haven't had any luck so far." It was true as far as it went: having made no effort to find his son, he had, not surprisingly, failed to do so. He steeled himself for the answer and asked the question that mattered most to him. "How much time are we talking, doctor?"

The oncologist blinked behind his glasses and screwed up his face in concentration while he tried to decide whether and how much to sugarcoat his answer.

Wynn waited impassively.

Apparently deciding that he was faced with a patient who wanted to hear it straight, he choked out an answer. "Um, I'd say anywhere between six weeks to four months. But bear in mind that we'd have to transfer your care to a center that performs the surgery, and those arrangements could take some time. So I'd encourage you not to delay." The doctor delivered the death sentence and stared across the room at Wynn.

Wynn nodded, immediately and with a force he didn't feel. "Thanks, Doc."

He carefully eased his swollen, sore feet into the slipper-like work shoes he'd found on the Internet. Then he straightened his shoulders and reached out his right hand. The doctor squeezed it gingerly.

As he shuffled out the door, the man called after him in a strangled voice, "Stop by Marie's desk and make an appointment for two weeks from now. Let her know if you need any refills on your medication. And Mr. Wynn?"

"Yeah?" Wynn turned slowly and peered at the doctor through narrowed eyes.

"I don't know your faith, sir. But it's never too late to pray for a miracle."

~ ~ ~ ~ ~ ~ ~ ~ ~ ~

It's never too late to pray for a miracle. The phrase reverberated in Wynn's ears all throughout the long journey back to his home. It rumbled through his brain as the cab driver slowly wended his way through crosstown Portland traffic to the bus depot.

It rattled in time with the wheels on the old bus as he bumped along to the ferry, lulling him into a fitful sleep that dredged up memories he'd rather not relive.

It echoed as he bounced in his seat as the boat churned through the choppy water to the island.

And it repeated rhythmically, like a drumbeat, while he drove his old dirty Jeep out of town and along the poorly maintained roads that wound their way from the highway to his compound.

Doug Wynn was not a man who counted on miracles. He hadn't survived this long by praying or hoping or waiting. He was a man who made things happen.

He had made his own luck his entire life. Now it looked like he would need to make his own miracle.

He unlocked the door to his home, shrugged out of his heavy parka, and warmed a can of soup to take the chill out of his bones. Then he waited for his nausea to pass, picked up the phone and dialed a number he'd hoped he'd never need to call.

"Yeah?" Stevey Tran answered on the second ring. His high-pitched, nasal voice, so incongruent to his height and bulk, was cautious and suspicious.

Wynn understood. Only a handful of men knew the telephone number he'd just dialed to reach Tran. And none of them would use it for anything less than a disaster. They'd vowed to cut their ties as a matter of survival.

"It's me. Duc." His tripped a bit over his birth name.

"What's wrong?"

"I need to find my son."

"That's not a good idea. You can't get sentimental in your old age. It's not safe."

Wynn snorted. "I'm not getting misty-eyed, you fool. I'm dying."

There was a long pause. When Tran spoke again, his voice was thick with emotion. "I'm sorry." He coughed. "But even so. Some things should go to the grave with us. Don't poke your head up."

"I have liver cancer, Stevey. I need a transplant. And I need it from a living donor. Someone compatible. So I thought ..."

"They can do that? Take out someone's liver and give it to you? Won't your kid die?"

To his surprise, the answer to that no. When the oncologist had first mentioned the possibility of a living donor, Wynn had asked the same question. As it turned out, the liver was unique in its ability to regenerate.

"No. They take, I don't know, half of it. And then the half in me grows to full-size and the one still in him grows back, too. He'd be good as new in a couple months." And I'd be alive, he added.

Tran squeaked out an appreciative whistle. "Science, man. That's unreal."

"Yeah." Wynn waited.

"But, still. That's a big ask. You know, for a kid who's never even met you."

"I'm his father." Wynn clenched his fist.

Tran sighed heavily. "It's risky, Duc."

Wynn said nothing. It had been decades since he'd seen the man. Stevey Tran, despite his size, was nothing but a bean counter. He'd kept the trains running on time, as the saying went. Wynn had been the muscle. And unless Stevey's memory had faded, he'd recall that nothing gave Wynn more pleasure than delivering a beating to some slow-to-pay debtor or reluctant shopkeeper. And his joy had extended to meting out discipline within the organization.

"I'll have to do some digging. It's been years since he popped up on the radar. Give me some time."

"Don't take too long. The doctors say I don't have much time left."

"Okay. I'll be in touch. Take care of yourself. And, Duc—?"

"Yes?"

"No fear, eh?"

"No fear," Wynn echoed before ending the call.

He pushed up his flannel shirt sleeve and traced the faded tattoo on the inside of his forearm: a small coffin, three candles, and the stylized letters *B.T.K. No fear,* he thought. He'd been so young that night in the Chinatown tattoo parlor when he imprinted his arm with the bravado that he was so tough he could face death unafraid. He stared for a moment at his sagging, wrinkled flesh and the distorted image on his arm—his rapid weight loss from treatment had left his skin hanging loosely from his frame like a too-large suit.

After a moment, he yawned and pushed himself up from the chair. The too-frequent trips to the mainland for medical appointments were getting harder. He wasn't willing to sacrifice his solitude for convenience. Not yet, at least.

He turned out the light and began the slow climb up the stairs to his bedroom.

No fear.

3.

SASHA STARED AT THE ELECTRONIC research database company's sales representative and willed him to wrap it up already. She still wasn't sure how he'd managed to worm his way onto her daily calendar, but he had. Her phone had beeped a reminder at her during her morning run and, sure enough, he'd arrived in her office with his rubber stress ball, fistful of free pens, and a laminated sheet listing all the new features of his company's program.

"Do you have any questions?" he asked, giving her an encouraging smile.

How do you keep your teeth so white? she wondered. But she didn't think that's what he had in mind.

"Does this plan include the practice guides and treatises?"

He bobbed his head. "Sure does."

"Okay, well, I'll hang on to this information and talk it over with—"

"Your partner. Of course."

"Actually, no. I'll talk it over with our legal assistant, er, our associate." She kept forgetting that Naya had passed the bar exam while she'd been out on maternity leave. Naya was a full-fledged attorney now. But she still did the bulk of the legal research—which meant she called the shots on the electronic database. If Will wanted to research something, he'd head out to one of the law school libraries and hunt through the stacks.

The rep began packing up his materials into his logo-branded computer bag. "Oh. I guess that makes more sense. It's just unusual for a firm to run that way."

She smiled. "We're an unusual firm, I guess." At that moment, her calendar chimed.

"Looks like we finished just in time," he joked. Then he shook her hand and let himself out.

He had no idea, she mused. If he thought McCandless & Volmer was unusual for consulting its employees on matters that involved them, it would probably blow his mind to know that her next meeting was with a pair of ravenous two-month olds.

As if on cue, Connelly swept into her office with Finn under one arm and Fiona under the other. Her twins squealed and gurgled when they saw her, and Finn gave her that smile that Connelly insisted was just gas.

"Hi." Connelly handed over Fiona and let the hiking backpack that he used for a diaper bag fall to the floor. Then he aimed a kiss in the general direction of Sasha's mouth.

"Hi, yourself, handsome." She took a moment to smile at her husband before she got busy feeding Fiona, while he took care of diapering Finn with quick, practiced motions.

Feeding time, bath time, every time had become a ballet, a *pas de deux*. Fiona ate her fill, and Sasha handed her to Connelly for burping and diapering while she picked up Finn and fed him.

"How's your morning going?" Connelly asked.

"So far, so good. Yours?"

"Great. I have a pan of lasagna in the works for tonight. I'm making an extra pan to freeze, too." He grinned at her.

Connelly was still officially on the federal government payroll in his unofficial capacity, reporting to Hank Richardson and his shadow agency. But Hank called on Connelly only when he needed him, so the highly trained federal agent with the top-secret clearances and sniper-level marksmanship skills spent his days going to pediatrician appointments, feeding the cat, walking the dog, and whipping up elaborate meals from scratch. And he seemed to love it.

"Fantastic. I'll pick up a bottle of red wine on my way home. I shouldn't be too late." She rubbed Finn's back until he rewarded her with a burp, then folded up the burp cloth she'd taken care to throw over her shoulder and slid it into her desk drawer. She'd learned that particular lesson the hard way.

"Don't bother stopping. I'll get it when we come back this afternoon for their high tea feeding."

She helped him gather the armloads of baby gear that were required for the shortest trip out of the house, then rocked the twins while he meticulously arranged the assorted baby gear so that it all fit in his backpack.

"See you later." She kissed each baby on the head and then stretched on her toes to kiss their father goodbye.

"Oh. I almost forgot. I got a letter from the DNA registry," Connelly said.

"And?"

He shook his head. "Dead end. No matches."

She stared into his gray eyes, trying to get a read on his emotions. "I'm sorry, babe."

He shrugged. "Like I said before, I've made my peace with never knowing who my father was. I'm just sorry Fiona and Finn will grow up with that question mark hanging over them." His voice was casual, but his mouth was a hard line.

"Hey, don't say that. We've only just gotten started searching for your dad. Maybe we should think about going to Vietnam in the spring, when the babies are a little older. Things have changed since the 80s. They may have better records than they did when you went looking for him."

His cheek muscle twitched, and she thought he was about to reject the idea out of hand. But he paused and then said, "Maybe. I was also thinking we could ask Naya to do an online search. She's pretty good at tracking down people who don't want to be found."

That wasn't a half-bad idea. Assuming Naya had the time. "Good thinking."

He smiled and planted another kiss near her ear. Then, as her intercom buzzed, he whisked the babies out of the office, intent on getting them home before they fell into their milk-induced slumber.

"Yes?" she said into the speaker as she smiled at her husband's departing back.

"Sorry to bother you with the babies in there," Caroline said apologetically, "but I have a Dr. Kayser on the line for you. He says it's important."

"It's no bother—Connelly's on his way out now. Go ahead and put the call through," Sasha assured her secretary.

As Caroline transferred the call, Sasha wondered what Dr. Kayser needed. He'd been her grandmother's physician when she'd been alive, and after her death, he'd helped Sasha with a case involving an elderly man who'd been improperly declared incapacitated. But it had been several years since she'd spoken to the geriatric doctor.

"Dr. Kayser, what a nice surprise," she said when she heard him on the line.

"Well, you may not think so after I tell you what I want." His voice boomed in her ear.

She sensed the joviality was forced, so she skipped the small talk. "What's going on?"

"Do you know the assisted living facility in Oakland called Golden Village?"

"I don't think so."

"It's one of those complexes that offers apartments and cottages for folks who are still able to live independently as well as nursing home care for those who can't."

"Okay, sure." Her nana had lived in her Squirrel Hill apartment until she'd died, but many of her old friends and neighbors had moved into facilities like the one Dr. Kayser was describing.

"I have so many patients who live out there now, that I've started making house calls there at least once a week—saves them a trip."

"A doctor who makes house calls? What year is it?"

He chuckled, but the laughter faded quickly. "Heh. In any event, several of my patients have finished out their lives in the locked dementia ward."

"How sad."

"It is," he agreed. "Losing one's mind ... well, it's an unpleasant end."

She listened to him shuffle some papers and clear his throat. Finally, he continued, "I think there's something untoward going on at Golden Village."

"Untoward?"

"Yes. I—well, I don't know exactly what's going on. But I thought back to Jed Craybill and how you helped him, and I thought you might be able to help me, too. Are you free for lunch today, by chance?"

No, she thought, she most definitely was not. She'd taken to working through lunch at her desk, eating whatever salad or soup Jake's had to offer. It was a bad habit, but it allowed her to eat dinner with Connelly and play with the babies before their bath time and bedtime. But she owed Dr. Kayser, even if he was too polite and well-bred to point it out.

"Yes," she said, "let's get lunch."

4.

THE DOORBELL CHIMED, once, then a second time, echoing through the quiet house and filling Leo with equal parts disbelief and irritation. He dried his hands on the dishtowel and hustled from the kitchen to the front of the house to answer the door before the caller could ring the bell again. The cat raced along beside him.

"This better not wake up the babies," he hissed to Java.

The cat mewed his agreement.

Leo didn't know what logistics were involved in getting one infant to nap, but getting two to nap at the same time required the alignment of the sun and the moon, a ton of luck, and the cooperation of family, friends, and delivery people who were willing to leave packages on the porch without ringing the doorbell. Whoever was out there better have a blasted good reason for being there.

He yanked the door open to find a skinny Asian kid shuffling his feet from side to side. The guy looked to be young, maybe twenty, and, if Leo were pressed to guess his ethnicity, he'd say Chinese. The kid was tall, almost as tall as Leo, but he rounded his bony shoulders forward and sort of stooped as if he were trying to take up no more space than was strictly necessary.

Leo took note of the guy's stiff, ill-fitting suit and the long hair, swooping over his eyes, and tried to peg the nervous young man. Salesman? Volunteer for a political candidate? Census taker?

"Can I help you?"

"Are you, uh, Leonard Connelly?"

"Depends who wants to know." Leo didn't know why he was even bothering to give the innocuous-looking guy a hard time. Habit, most likely.

The guy blinked rapidly, waiting for Leo to elaborate.

When he didn't, he squeaked out an answer, "I'm a ... messenger. There's a gentleman in Maine who has information about your father." He sing-songed the sentence in a rushed, high-pitched voice, as if he'd memorized the line and wanted to get it out of his mouth before he forgot it or screwed it up.

His father?

Leo's pulse ticked up a notch and his mouth went dry. He forced himself to stay composed. He steadied his breathing and cleared his throat.

"My father?" He asked the question as if he were only mildly curious about the response.

"Yeah. The gentleman in Maine says he can put you in touch with your dad. Uh, if you want."

The kid waited, looking at him with an expectant expression. Leo stepped out onto the porch and stood close to the messenger, deliberately crowding the kid just a bit.

"Who's this gentleman?"

The boy tripped back a step, putting a little distance between him and Leo. "His name's Mr. Wynn. Here—" He fumbled with gloved hands in his jacket pocket and pulled out a crumpled business envelope. He lunged forward and pressed the envelope into Leo's hands. Then he turned and hurried down the stairs to the sidewalk.

Leo stood, oblivious to the cold wind swirling around his bare ankles, and watched the guy trot to the corner and cross the street. The kid craned his neck over his shoulder and saw Leo still standing on the porch. He broke into a full run.

Either by design or whim of the urban parking gods, his visitor hadn't parked in sight of the house, so Leo couldn't get a look at his vehicle. He almost started after the guy but remembered the two sleeping infants inside. After a moment, he turned and walked back into the house in a daze.

He lowered himself onto the leather couch and stared at the unaddressed envelope. After a moment, he slit the top open with his fingernail. He shook out a piece of lined loose-leaf paper.

Someone had printed in careful block letters a name and address of sorts:

DOUG WYNN

THE BLUE HOUSE

GREAT CRANBERRY ISLAND, MAINE

Beneath the address, there was a single sentence printed in the same block lettering:

COME ON OCTOBER 22ND.

That was it. The note, such as it was, was unsigned. He turned the paper over in his hands taking care to touch it as little as possible. The reverse side was blank. He sat there for a long time, listening to the mantle clock's gentle ticking, until Mocha wandered into the room and nudged his leg. He reached down with one hand and absentmindedly scratched the dog's ears for a while.

Then, holding the paper by one corner, he headed to the office to make a photocopy.

His father was alive. After all this time, his father was alive, and Doug Wynn, whoever he was, might know where to find him.

5.

THE ROOM BEGAN TO TILT. Greta Allstrom gripped the edge of the metal lab table and steadied herself. Heat crept from her hairline to her toes and her vision blurred and then faded, as the corners of the room grew dark. She focused on not panting, forcing herself to take deep, slow breaths until her heart rate slowed and her vision cleared.

When the moment of lightheadedness passed, she let go of the table and shook out her hands. Then she stood cautiously and walked slowly across the lab room to the metal filing cabinet where she stashed her handbag each day. She opened the bottom drawer and removed a spotted banana, an energy bar, and a bottle of water.

She wolfed down the bar and banana and tossed the wrapper and peel in the biohazardous waste bin that served as her trash can. Then she drank the lukewarm water in one long gulp and aimed the empty bottle at the recycling basket.

You can't forget to eat, she scolded herself as she hurried back to the table. Eating, while time-consuming and inefficient, was an unfortunate, but necessary, interruption to her work.

She traced the scar that lined her cheek, a reminder of the day last month that she'd passed out from hunger. She'd been about to make a breakthrough and had been working for more than forty-hours in an adrenaline- and caffeine-fueled session, when suddenly she'd grown dizzy. She'd hit her face on a stack of glass specimen slides as she collapsed and had awoken in a slick pool of blood. The resultant stitches and completion of the obligatory OSHA incident report had eaten up more time than a quick meal break would have.

Ever since, she'd vowed to pay closer attention to her body's needs and, so far, had avoided a repeat performance. She couldn't afford to lose any more lab time. Not when she was *this* close to a breakthrough. Not when the Alpha Fund was waiting for a progress report.

She adjusted her safety goggles and peered into the microscope. She was scouring the blood smears on the slides for hypersegmented neutrophils. A normal mature neutrophil would typically have three or four segments, or nuclear lobes. If a cell contained six or more lobes, it fit the clinical definition of hypersegmentation, a symptom of cobalamine, or Vitamin B12, deficiency. The samples she reviewed often contained as many as eight or even ten lobes.

She was counting under her breath and didn't hear the door swing open, so she nearly knocked over her specimen when Troy Norman, one of her graduate students, coughed just over her left shoulder. She started and turned.

"So sorry, Dr. Allstrom. I didn't mean to startle you." He smiled sheepishly.

"You didn't," she lied even though he obviously had. "Do you have the samples?"

He nodded and passed her a soft-sided cooler bag, like the ones office workers use to keep their lunches chilled. Just knowing that now, at this moment, she held in her hands the tissue samples she needed to test her hypothesis filled her with a warm, pervasive sense of peace and calm.

"Do you need any help?" he asked with the eagerness of a puppy.

She didn't. But she prided herself on being a mentor to the promising students who chose to commit to the grueling schedule she demanded.

She'd think of some task that would engage him without endangering her work.

"Yes, please stay."

He dragged a high metal stool across the floor and perched on it immediately, as if he feared she might change her mind if he took too long.

"What are you doing now?"

"I'm comparing the samples from the controls with the hyperhomocysteinemiac group who received the supplement."

The supplement. It sounded so innocuous, like an over-the-counter concoction of herbs that a person might buy at her local pharmacy, not quite believing it would work. But *this* supplement was a powerful blend of B-vitamins and fatty acids that were often deficient in dementia patients. The working hypothesis had long been that coblamine deficiency was responsible for demyelination of the myelin sheath and that the sheath could be repaired through nutrition, supplements, and perhaps, someday, prescription drugs. None of this was particularly cutting edge.

"And the tissues?" Norman asked. "We'll thinslice those to confirm that the supplement did help to regenerate the sheath?"

"We hope."

"And then ... the nano-robotics team can start its trials?"

"Soon. We just need a healthy control slice."

The nano-robotics team, *there* was the cutting edge.

Greta had long suspected that the supplement would work better if it were delivered in massive quantities directly to a patient's glial cells, where the myelin sheath was formed. But how to get it there? The answer had come to her on a rare evening off while she was watching *Innerspace* on late-night cable, marveling at how a movie about a miniaturized Dennis Quaid being trapped inside Martin Short had managed to net an Oscar. And then it hit her. A surgeon could insert a nano-robot into a patient's body and, using a simple joystick, remotely guide the tiny robot to the glial cells, where it would coat the cells with her supplement. She'd been so excited that she'd headed straight into the lab at one o'clock in the morning to flesh out her idea without even bothering to change out of her pajamas first.

Nearly a year had passed since her brainstorm—a mere blip in time in the institutional research world, but to Greta it felt like an eternity. Each day that passed had seemed to her to be a failure, a missed opportunity. So she worked, harder, faster, committed to bringing her cure to fruition.

News of her work had spread through the scientific and technological communities, and she'd been offered a plum speaking engagement at a joint conference put on by MIT and Harvard. That had resulted in an infusion of cash from the Alpha Fund.

And now her borderline harebrained notion was *this close* to reality. If the brain tissue samples showed that the supplement had even a small positive effect, then the next stage—the nano-robotics phase—would go into production just as soon as she had a healthy brain tissue slice to use as the standard. She was convinced—certain to her core—that if her nano-robots became a reality, the horrifying specter of cognitive degeneration would someday be nothing more than a historical footnote. She prayed she was right. Otherwise the Faustian bargain she'd struck with the Alpha Fund had been for nothing.

6.

SASHA WATCHED DR. KAYSER methodically cut his grilled salmon into bite-sized pieces and mix the fish into his large salad. Then he arranged the little ceramic bowl of dressing just so onto the side of his plate and looked up at her.

"Aren't you hungry?" he asked, nodding his head toward her stew.

"Just waiting for it to cool down a bit."

He smiled, blinked behind his glasses, and scanned the room.

The restaurant was nearly empty—the noon rush was long over, the lunchtime crowd back in their offices. The only other patrons were a cluster of business suits at the bar.

He took a bite of salad, chewed, swallowed, and dabbed at his mouth with the corner of his napkin. They'd exhausted the social topics—the twins, his health, the Steelers—it was time to get to the point of their meeting. But she'd learned long ago never to rush a witness. He'd start his story when he was ready. She eyed her bowl again, but it was still steaming. So she folded her hands in her lap and waited.

He repeated the bite, chew, swallow, dab routine and sipped his water. Then he rested his fork on the edge of his plate and leaned forward.

Here we go.

"It probably comes as no surprise to you that many of my patients—maybe most of them—end up losing their minds at the end of their lives. Dementia is terrifying to think about, but in some ways, if a person lives long enough, it becomes almost inevitable."

Sasha's mouth quirked into a little frown of disagreement, but she said nothing.

Across the table, Dr. Kayser must have noted her skepticism. He nodded. "Yes, your grandmother was the exception to that rule. She was one of the lucky ones. Her mind was as sharp the day she died as it was the day I met her. But you can't count on being so lucky. So one thing I do at the very first patient visit is explain the process of cognitive deterioration. It's important for people to understand the possibility that there will come a day when they'll no longer be able to recognize their husbands and wives and children, drive a car, or balance a checkbook. They need to make their end of life decisions and plans while they still can. It's not a pleasant topic, to be sure, but it's a critical one."

Sasha stared at the doctor's ordinarily jovial face, now so somber. She didn't envy him having those conversations. "Of course," she said, prompting him to continue.

"I encourage all of my patients to consider enrolling in research studies to find causes and cures of early-onset dementia, Alzheimer's disease, Parkinson's disease, and other cognitive neuropathies—regardless of whether they're exhibiting any signs of dementia or have family histories—"

"Hang on. Once a person's showing signs of cognitive impairment, he or she doesn't really have the capacity to enroll in a study. Right?"

He cut another piece of salmon into a small bite but left it on his plate. "You're thinking of our friend, Mr. Craybill, aren't you?"

"I am." They'd worked together on behalf of a man who had been deemed incompetent by a local welfare agency. A finding of incapacitation meant he wasn't competent to give consent.

"Well, as I understand it, there are different standards for consent under the law and under medical ethics. And it's possible for a person to provide informed consent to medical research even if he's already been diagnosed with diminished capacity. You're right, though, that it's much cleaner to enroll in a study when you have full possession of your faculties. In fact, that's what your grandmother did."

"She did?"

"Yes. She enrolled in a brain study where she spent 30 minutes a week doing puzzles and playing memory and spatial games online. She was in the control group."

Sasha smiled. "I remember Nana's games. She loved them. I didn't realize they were part of a study; I thought she was just keeping her knives honed, as she liked to say."

That elicited a small chuckle from the doctor. "Yes, it's been shown that doing crossword puzzles and playing cognitive games does keep the brain healthy. Not everyone stays quite as sharp as she did, but, if nothing else, those activities will slow the decline. In any case, I make sure all my patients are aware of the various studies into the aging brain. I believe that's one of my duties as someone who specializes in treating an aging population."

"Sounds reasonable," Sasha agreed.

He smiled again, a little sadly this time. "It does sound reasonable, doesn't it? And I truly thought I was doing a service to my patients. Now, I'm not so sure." His eyes dropped to the table.

"Why's that?"

He looked up. "How much do you know about informed consent in the context of medical research?"

Sasha considered the question. "I'm not sure," she admitted after a moment. "I have a pretty solid grasp of the concept of informed consent with regard to medical *treatment*. I know a physician is required to explain a procedure to a patient; give the patient complete information about the risks and benefits of a procedure, as well as the alternatives to the procedure; and ensure that the patient is in fact providing consent to the procedure before taking any action."

The doctor nodded. "Yes, yes, that's all right. Medical research is a little bit different, however, in that the requirement for obtaining consent is governed by federal regulation and compliance is tied to funding for the research. Screw up on the consent part, and a researcher risks losing federal dollars."

"Serious stuff." She picked up her spoon and tackled her autumn stew while he educated her on the finer points.

"Indeed. Typically, there will be an IRB, or institutional review board, overseeing the consent process and the entire study. It's quite formal and structured."

"That all sounds like a good thing," Sasha remarked.

"I've always thought so, too, particularly because, thanks to my efforts, many of my patients are enrolled in various research studies. Most of them are run through the local universities and hospitals, but not all of them. But I've always had the peace of mind that the participants' interests were being protected. Until now."

"What's changed?" Sasha probed, sneaking a discreet peek at her watch. She didn't want to rush the doctor but at the same time she had a packed schedule and two babies who would be looking for their afternoon snack in about an hour.

"What's changed is that I think one major local study is playing fast and loose with the rules," he said in a slow, halting voice. "There's a study led by a woman named Greta Allstrom—she's very well-regarded, a real up and comer. She works closely with Golden Village's dementia unit. Her research team goes over and performs regular blood draws

on residents who previously consented to participate in her study, including many of my patients."

He paused again, and Sasha told herself to be
patient, wait him out.

He pushed the greens around on his plate for a
moment. Then he looked up and said, "I believe Dr.
Allstrom's gone too far. Not surprisingly, I've had a
number of patients pass on while living at Golden
Village. That is, after all, the point of such a facility.
Since July, four of my patients who were enrolled
in the study and residents in the dementia unit
have died. As their treating physician, I was called
in when they died."

Sasha wasn't quite following his train of
thought, but her imagination was working over-
time. "And you suspect foul play?"

"Oh, goodness, no. Nothing like that. But something untoward's going on." He removed his napkin from his lap, draped it over his half-eaten salad,
then pushed the plate away. "I find it important to
the family for me to stay involved in the process
even after the death certificate has been signed. Often times, I've treated their loved one for years. My
bearing witness to the end of life—attending the
services, sharing stories—I think it helps give some
closure."

Sasha flashed back to the Irish wake her family
had held for her Russian grandmother. Dr. Kayser

had shown up and joined right in, telling uproarious stories that left her brothers laughing and even brought a smile to her mother's lips.

"Of course." She nodded and waited for him to continue.

"At first, I didn't think anything of it. But these patients each had brain tissue removed during their autopsies."

"That's not standard?"

"Not really. Some people do donate their brains to science, but I asked some discreet questions of the next of kin. None of the four had done so. Their brain matter was harvested without consent."

The statement hung in the air over the table for a long, silent moment.

"Are you sure?"

"I wasn't but I am now. All four patients had enrolled in Dr. Allstrom's study; as part of the research protocol, all four patients did have regular blood draws; but not one of them had consented to the study of their brain tissue postmortem."

He looked at her expectantly, waiting for her to solve this problem or tell him what to do.

"Could a family member have consented just before or right after death?"

"That's what I thought, too, until I started asking questions. That's not what happened here. They're taking brain tissue without permission. And I need you to help me stop them."

7.

SASHA BURST THROUGH THE FRONT door and closed it quickly against the wind. As she hung her coat in the hall closet, she inhaled deeply. The smell of garlic bread baking and the spicy aroma of Connelly's pasta sauce permeated the house, leading her to the warm, brightly lit kitchen.

Connelly was mixing a green salad and Finn and Fiona were side-by-side on their red, black, and white baby mats, staring up at the developmentally appropriate toys dangling overhead, reaching their little arms toward the mobiles and cooing. She wasn't entirely convinced that babies could only see red, white, and black but she was pretty sure it was true of dogs. Mocha loved the mat and was forever trying to claim it as his napping spot. Even now, he was stretched out on the floor with his paws on the edge of the mat, waiting for his chance to weasel his way onto it.

Everyone except the dog turned at the sound of her heels clicking across the floor. She crouched to nuzzle the babies' soft fuzzy heads in greeting. Connelly walked over and handed her a glass of wine. "Hi." he said, giving her a quick kiss.

"Sorry I'm late." She smiled sheepishly as she accepted the glass and leaned into him.

She was sorry. Her lunch with Dr. Kayser had run longer than she'd planned, and when she returned to the office she found herself distracted by his story. Her mind kept returning to his patients and their families and the abuse of trust they may have suffered. As a result, she hadn't been particularly productive.

"Everything okay?" Connelly asked as if he had read her mind—or more likely her expression.

"Just a long day. I'll hurry up and change and then feed the wonder twins before dinner."

For their part, the babies had switched their attention from the mobiles to the conversation going on above their heads. Their eyes were volleying back and forth between Sasha and Connelly as if they were watching a tennis match.

"Sounds good," he said. Then he turned to the twins. "Come on, team, tummy time while mummy changes," he cooed as he flipped them onto their stomachs. They both eked out cranky howls of protest.

"You monster," she teased over her shoulder. He gave her a crooked smile and turned back to his salad while she hurried upstairs, wineglass in hand, and traded her high heels, dress, and suit jacket for a pair of comfortable yoga pants and a soft, slouchy top.

By the time she said hello to the cat sleeping insolently on her cashmere sweater and padded back downstairs, Connelly had set the table. She eyed the twins and judged Finn to be the sleepier of the two. So she sat at the kitchen table and fed him first, while Connelly bustled around putting the finishing touches on his meal one-handed while Fiona clung to him like a small monkey. Finn's eyelids drooped, then fluttered, then closed. She kissed him then traded him off to Connelly to transfer him to bed and took Fiona in her arms. Her daughter gazed up at her with an expression that seemed to indicate she thought her brother was a sucker for missing out on this grown-up time.

When Sasha had returned to work full-time a few weeks ago, the kids had naturally fallen into a routine that ensured everyone got plenty of one-on-one time (well, everyone except for her and

Connelly). Finn, who was the night owl of the pair fell asleep before dinner and then was awake in the late evening. Fiona usually joined her parents at the table and then fell asleep shortly after, slumbering through Finn's midnight escapades. The differences in her twins were almost as amazing as the similarities.

As she fed Fiona, she asked, "Can I do anything to help?"

"Sit. Eat," he responded. He brought the salad bowl and warm bread to the table and sat across from her.

She smiled at him over Fiona's head. "What did I do to deserve you?"

"I don't know. But whatever your sin was, maybe you can make amends in your next life." He winked.

She laughed at that, and so did Fiona as if she got the joke, too.

"How'd it go today? Did you get to talk to Dr. Kayser?" he asked as he passed her the salad bowl.

Sasha frowned. "I did. He's concerned about some of his patients—for good reason."

"What's the issue?" Connelly asked.

"I'll know more after I meet with some of his patients, but there's a chance that some researchers may be taking advantage of dementia patients to avoid getting informed consent."

"That sounds ... ugly."

"It feels ugly, too. Let's talk about something else. Was your day interesting?"

A shadow crossed his face and he took a sip of wine before answering. "You could say that."

Something in his tone sent a shiver of worry down her spine. She waited for him to continue.

"I had an unexpected visitor today."

"Was it my mom again?" She tensed her shoulders. She thought she'd finally convinced Valentina that Connelly really was more than capable of taking care of the kids while she was at work.

"It wasn't your mom. It was a messenger."

"You mean, a delivery service or something?"

"No. Here. Don't worry, this is a photocopy. I'm going to give Hank the original and ask him to check it for prints." Connelly reached into his pocket and removed a square of paper. He passed it across the table to her.

She carefully unfolded the sheet of paper and stared down at the printing. "Who's Doug Wynn?"

"I don't know, but he claims to have information about my father." His face was drawn, his expression unreadable.

"Your father? Are you sure?"

He shook his head. "I'm not. I haven't had a chance to look into this guy's background yet. The kids woke up just after his messenger left, and they kept me hopping. I'm going to talk to Hank tomorrow and have him run this guy through the databases. I mean, this could be a shakedown."

"It could be," she said slowly, "but you haven't been really public about the fact the you're looking for him. I mean, there's no reward or anything for information."

"True. But maybe someone hacked the files at the DNA registry and is trying to prey on orphans desperate to make a connection."

"Maybe. Or it could be legit." He shrugged but made the concession in a tone that suggested it pained him to do so.

Then her imagination ran ahead of her and she tightened her grip on the baby reflexively. "Or it could be an ambush. I guess we've made enough enemies that it would pay to be careful."

"Agreed. Like I said, I'll talk to Hank in the morning."

She studied her husband's grim face for a long moment. "You know, you can allow yourself to feel a little bit of excitement. This Doug Wynn guy might turn out to be a dead end, but he also might have a solid lead. Imagine if this guy actually does know where your dad is?"

He took his time answering. "Let's not get ahead of ourselves."

"You're right." She knew him well enough to know he'd need time to get used to the idea that this might be the way to learn about his past. There was no point in pushing the issue.

He looked as if he were about to say something more, but before he had the chance, Fiona pitched forward and her little fists went straight down in the middle of Sasha's plate of lasagna. Pasta sauce splashed in the air and rained down over the three of them and all over the table.

8.

EO LOOKED AROUND HANK RICHARDS' makeshift office. As befit the director of a secretive, shadow agency, Hank had no permanent office. The government rented space for him on an as-needed basis through a series of boring-sounding covers. For instance, anyone sufficiently curious about who was leasing the six hundred square feet on the ground floor of the Grant Street building to do any research into the matter would learn that the lessee was the dry-sounding Assistant Secretary for Administration and Management for the Department of Labor. At that point, Leo was sure, the intrepid researcher would move on to a more interesting pastime—say, watching paint dry or clipping his or her toenails.

"Nice digs."

Hank smirked. "It gets the job done. You try accomplishing anything with six kids roaming through the house."

"I can only imagine." Finn and Fiona weren't even mobile yet, and he couldn't see how he'd plan any effective, shady covert operations with them around.

"Speaking of kids, where are they?"

"Sasha's mom's watching them. They don't care much for meetings."

Hank nodded sagely. "Smart kids. I don't care much for them either." He gestured toward an industrial-looking metal chair. "Make yourself comfortable, to the extent you can. And tell me what's going on."

Leo lowered himself into the hard chair and got right to the point. "I need a favor."

"I'm listening." Hank rested his forearms on the desk and leaned forward.

"Can you run a name for me?" Leo opened a manila envelope. He removed the sheet of paper bearing Doug Wynn's name and address and passed it across the desk to Hank.

Hank held the paper by its edges and peered down at it. "Who's Doug Wynn?"

"That's what I want to know. I can access some of the records myself, but what I really need is a complete, exhaustive search that includes all the databases I don't even know about."

Leo had worked for the government in enough unofficial capacities to suspect that there were databases so secret even he didn't have clearance to access them. Hank's chuckle confirmed his guess.

"Wanna tell me why? You don't have to."

Leo met Hank's clear, brown eyes with a level gaze. "He may have information about my father." He could tell by the way Hank jerked his head back that he hadn't expected that response.

"Your dad?"

"Maybe."

Hank examined his fingernails for a moment before squinting at Leo. "You know we ran all the available information about your father through all the databases, including the ones that may or may not exist, before we ever hired you?"

"I know."

"And you probably know I've updated that search from time to time, seeing as how you're one of my contractors."

"I assumed as much."

"And the combined forces of the United States government know diddly squat about your father."

"I know that, too." His jaw tensed involuntarily, and he reached up with one hand and turned his chin until he heard a satisfying *crack*.

Hank winced. "I thought Sasha told you to stop doing that. She'd be mad as a wet hen if she knew you were still cracking your jaw."

"Then don't tell her." He grinned at Hank for a moment and then got serious. "I know you hit a dead end with my dad. So did I. So did the Vietnamese Orphan DNA Registry."

"So what's this all about?"

"That's what I need to know. Some guy showed up at my house yesterday, handed me an envelope that had this piece of paper in it, and told me this Wynn guy has information about my dad." He felt his jaw clench again but resisted the urge to release it manually. "Anyway, I need to know if there's anything to it—or if it's a shakedown or what. Oh, and maybe run that for prints, if you can?"

Hank shook his head slowly. "Gee, I never would have thought of that, ace. But seriously, I don't like this. How'd this guy find you? Who was this messenger?"

"No clue. The twins were sleeping. He gave me the note and bolted from the porch. I couldn't go after him, but I don't think he knew anything. He was young, nervous. An Asian guy."

Hank quirked an eyebrow at that. "Vietnamese?"

"I don't think so. Chinese, if I had to guess."

"Huh."

"Yeah. Anyway, I don't know how this Wynn guy tracked me down, and I don't like that at all. Sasha's got Naya working that angle. I need to find out everything I can about Wynn in the next week."

Hank's head snapped up. "You aren't really thinking about going up to Maine? That's foolhardy."

"Maybe it is, maybe it isn't. I guess it depends on what you find out."

Hank sighed heavily, like a man used to having weight on his shoulders, which is what he was. "Do you still have the envelope?"

Leo took it from his jacket pocket and handed it to Hank, who grasped the edge of the envelope with two fingers. "My prints are all over it. I tried to be more careful with the note."

"It'll take a few days, but I'll find out everything I can about your Mr. Wynn." He stood and gave Leo a reassuring look.

Leo opened his mouth to thank his friend and sometimes employer and was surprised to find his words caught in his throat. He coughed. "I appreciate it, Hank."

Hank clasped a big hand on Leo's shoulder. "No thanks needed, son."

Leo nodded and stared at Hank. He wanted to say something more, something about how he considered Hank a mentor, almost a father, but the lump in his throat made it impossible to get the words out.

Hank gave Leo a look that seemed to say he knew what Leo was thinking. Then he shooed him out of the dreary office.

~ ~ ~ ~ ~ ~ ~ ~ ~ ~

"Can you do me a favor?" Sasha asked, popping her head into Naya's office on her way back from her mid-morning visit to the coffee shop.

Naya marked her spot on the documents she was reviewing with one finger and glanced up. "Depends on the favor."

"Fair enough. I need to find out how someone could track down Connelly."

She was careful to keep her tone light and casual, but Naya wasn't fooled. She narrowed her almond-shaped eyes and gave Sasha a close look. "Track him down how?"

Sasha stepped into the room and pulled the door shut behind her before answering. "I know property records are searchable, but given, uh, our history, we set up a trust to buy the new house. So, anyone searching tax records or the sales database should have found Java and Mocha Trust, LLC as the buyer."

"You named your trust after your pets?" Naya cracked.

"Don't judge. And focus, please."

Naya shook her head but said, "Okay, go on."

"Now, I know I'm listed as the seller of my condo, but that wouldn't give anyone a trail to find my new address, right? And, we're obviously not listed in the phone book. So, how would someone—a stranger—show up on my front porch looking for Connelly?"

Naya scrunched her face up into an expression of consternation. "What kind of stranger?"

"No clue. He said he was a messenger on behalf of a guy who has information about Connelly's father."

The legal assistant's eyebrows rocketed up her forehead. "Leo's dad?"

"I know, right? This could be great. Or ..."

"It could be a trap." Naya filled in the words that Sasha was loath to say.

"Right."

Naya thought for a long moment. "I don't know. I can poke around some in the publicly available databases, see if I can put together a bread crumb trail that leads to Leo. But if this guy has connections, he could have access to government databases or something that I don't."

Sasha chewed on her lower lip while she considered her course of action. "I can give you the guy's name. See what you can find out about him. But be really careful, please. If he *is* connected—either to friends or enemies of ours—he might find out you're looking and get spooked."

Naya waved away her concern. "Don't worry. I'm always careful. I assume Hank's also going to run him down?"

Sasha nodded. "He is. Connelly went to talk to him today. So, focus on figuring out how this guy, whoever he is, found us. But if you want to check him out too, the name is Doug Wynn. W-Y-N-N. And he apparently lives on Great Cranberry Island in Maine. I did some basic searches myself, but nothing popped."

"Well, now the experts are involved. Let me and Hank take care of it." Naya shot her a grin.

"Thanks, Nancy Drew." Sasha reached behind her for the door and then paused. "Oh, one more thing. This one's actually billable work. I'm heading over to Golden Village tomorrow morning to meet with the administrative director about Dr. Kayser's concerns. Want to come along?"

"Sure."

"Great. He's expecting us at ten o'clock."

"What should I do to prepare?" She pawed through the papers on her desk and unearthed a legal pad and pen.

"Get familiar with the federal regulations governing medical research and informed consent, but other than that, there's not much to do. I told Dr. Kayser I'd try a low-key approach and see if we can resolve this mess informally, so don't spend a ton of time on it until we know it's going to turn into something."

"You think this director is going to admit the research team screwed up and promise to make them stop?"

Naya's tone left no doubt as to her view of the likelihood of that outcome, but Sasha shrugged. "It could happen."

"When did you become such a pie-eyed optimist?"

"When I learned that I can, in fact, function on three hours of interrupted sleep each night. Anything's possible. The sky's the limit!" she trilled in an overly enthusiastic voice as she raised her coffee mug in a salute.

"You need a nap," Naya told her. Then she turned back to her reading.

9.

WYNN WATCHED FROM THE BIG bay window in his dining room while the kid dug a hole four feet deep and six feet long in the woods between the house and the coast. The young man whistled and sweated from the effort of breaking up the rocky Maine soil.

He pushed himself up from the chair. The hole was done. He pulled on his overcoat, fastened it to his chin, and then eased his hands into his leather gloves.

When he stepped out onto the back patio and shut the door, the kid twisted to look up at him from deep within the hole. "How's it look, Mr. Wynn?" he asked, flashing a proud, toothy smile.

Wynn shuffled closer and pretended to inspect the kid's handiwork. He gave a slow nod of approval. "It'll do. Thank you, son."

"You really gonna kill that Leonard Connelly dude, like you said, sir?"

That was the problem with these young kids. They couldn't just dig a grave because you told them to. They had to know what it was for. "As I said, it's a grave." He extended his hand, gesturing for the shovel.

The kid handed it over, and Wynn dropped it to the ground.

"Hey, give me a hand out of here, and I can put that back in your shed if you want."

"I'll take care of it. Oh, did you tell anyone about your trip to Pennsylvania?" He kept his voice mild, hoping he struck a note of idle curiosity.

The kid stroked his chin in thought. "No. I mean, nobody other than Mr. Tran."

Wynn wasn't worried about Stevey. He assumed Stevey had predicted the messenger's fate and had assigned the job to someone he considered to be expendable. And if he hadn't, well, that was Stevey's problem.

"Good."

The kid—Wynn realized he'd already forgotten his name—raised his right arm, waiting for Wynn to reach down and pull him out of the hole. "If you ever need anything else, Mr. Wynn, I'd be happy to help."

Wynn reached into his pocket and retrieved his handgun. He aimed for the heart and fired twice. The kid crumpled into the grave he'd dug himself. Wynn put the third and final bullet between the messenger's eyes.

"Nothing personal," he said as the light dimmed from the kid's eyes.

He waited a long moment to make sure the guy was dead before he bent and rifled through the corpse's pockets. He removed the keys to the Honda, the guy's wallet, and the roll of cash he'd handed over earlier in payment for services rendered. He stuffed the money into his pocket. He was breathing heavily from exertion and adrenaline but he still had work to do.

He'd made the kid dig his own grave--not out of cruelty, as he once would have, but out of sheer necessity. *But had he really needed to kill him?* The question snuck up on him.

Of course he had, he chided himself.

The fact that he even gave the matter a second thought was evidence that he was getting soft. And getting soft was an excellent way to get caught. No, eliminating the messenger was unavoidable. The kid could tie him to Leonard Connelly. And while reaching out to his son was a risk Wynn had had no choice but to take, there was no reason to be reckless about it.

It took him nearly an hour to shovel dirt over the dead man and fill the hole. He paused every few minutes to catch his breath, leaning heavily against the shovel. By the time he finished, the weak autumn sun was setting and he was wet with perspiration and chilled from the cool evening air.

Wynn wanted nothing more than to hobble into the house and crawl into his bed. But there was work still to be done. Thanks to the kid's laziness, he needed to drive the Civic that he'd stolen from the ferry parking lot into the tractor shed, away from curious eyes. He needed to start a fire and burn the wallet and its contents. He needed to take his medications and eat a meal.

The familiar rush that invariably came with taking a life had already dissipated, leaving him drained and weary. He sighed and trudged toward the car, cursing the fact that his messenger hadn't wanted to walk up the hill. Now he had to figure out how to deal with the stolen car.

10.

"REALLY?" Naya eyed Sasha as if she thought the suggestion to walk to the retirement center was an elaborate joke.

"Yes, really. Come on—it's not even a mile. It'll be good for both of us. And the weather's perfect for a brisk fall walk."

That was true—it was one of those glorious autumn days with abundant sunshine, crisp air, and not a cloud in sight.

Naya shifted her gaze to the large window behind her desk and shrugged. "It does look like a nice day," she conceded.

Sasha beamed at her. "Great. Grab your coat." She wrapped her scarf around her throat and hoisted her bag up onto her shoulder then followed Naya out of the office and down the stairs with a small smile. By the time Naya realized their route took them straight up Forbes, and the steep hill that was the bane of every high school cross-country runner in the city, it would be too late for her to dig in her heels. It would be an onward and upward situation.

As they stepped out onto the pavement, Naya turned and smirked at Sasha over her shoulder. "I know about the hill, Mac."

A bubble of laughter rose in Sasha's throat. "Oh. I'm glad to know you're undaunted."

"Of course I'm undaunted." Naya's gaze landed on Sasha's feet. "I'm not the one wearing ridiculous shoes."

"You're pronouncing adorable wrong," Sasha informed her as she turned her foot to show off the stacked four-inch heel. "Aren't these cute?"

Naya changed the subject. "Hey, I think I know how that Wynn guy found Leo."

Sasha stopped at the corner and pressed the button to activate the 'Walk' sign. "Really? Already?"

"Yep. Well, I think so, at least." She paused to let the suspense build.

The light changed, and Sasha stepped out into the street. "Tell me already."

"Well, here's my thinking. If this Wynn guy knows Leo's dad, the most he would know about

Leo is his mom's name and his approximate age, right?"

Sasha shifted the bag on her arm and considered the premise. "Probably."

"So I started by searching for information about her."

"Her? Leo's mother?"

"Right."

They started their trek up the sharp incline, and Sasha hustled to match Naya's long stride and drive home the point that she was in no way hobbled by her choice of fashionable footwear. "What did you find out?"

"Not a ton. You know, she's been dead for a long time. But, she left a digital trail of places they lived, hospitals where she worked, that sort of thing."

She nodded. Leo's mother had been a traveling nurse. She imagined her globetrotting had created a decent footprint. "And?"

"Well, her obituary's available online, and it says that she was survived by one son, Leonard Connelly. At that time, he was identified as living in Washington, D.C."

"So anyone who knew her name could find out his name."

"Right. But, I'm sure it comes as no shock that the trail kind of goes cold at Leo. I mean, his name pops up in newspaper articles about your, uh, adventures. But he's usually just listed as 'federal agent Leo Connelly' or something equally vague. No precise job title or department, let alone a personal residence. And he moved around a lot himself when he was with Homeland Security."

Naya was breathing harder now, which gratified Sasha just a bit because her feet were *killing* her. They were silent for a moment as they mounted the steepest part of the hill.

When they crested the top, Sasha said, "How's that get us to today?"

Naya gnawed on her lower lip.

"What?" Sasha pressed.

Naya stopped walking and faced Sasha squarely. "Your mom."

"My mom?" What could Valentina possibly have to do with any of this?

Naya gave a wry nod. "Yeah. When the twins were born, she donated altar flowers to her church in their honor."

That sounded like something her mother would do. "Okay? So?"

"So, in the September newsletter, St. Mark's listed Finn and Fiona's birthdate, your name and Leo's, and your current address in case anyone wanted to drop off a casserole or something."

"You're kidding."

"Did you get a lot of casseroles?"

"As a matter of fact, we did."

"Right. The newsletter for every month is archived on the church website as a PDF. It's the only place I found your current address and Leo's name. But it's not hard to find. I mean, if someone was searching for him, they could connect those dots."

They could and, apparently, did. Sasha was silent for a moment, lost in thought.

"It's an honest mistake, Mac."

Sasha jerked her head up and met Naya's eyes. "You mean my mom sharing our address? I know. I'm sure it seemed harmless to her."

Her mother didn't fully understand the fact that there were more than a few dangerous people who would love to know where Sasha and Connelly lived. She did understand a community coming together to support new parents, though. It was simply a function of her frame of reference.

"You could call the church and ask them to delete it."

She could and likely would. But the horse had already left the barn. Closing the door wasn't going to change anything. "Good idea. Thanks for running it down. Did you find out anything about this Wynn character?"

Naya shook her head forcefully. "Uh-uh. No. That guy is a cipher. Maybe Hank'll have better luck."

"Maybe."

They reached the wrought-iron gate that surrounded the manicured lawns of Golden Village and paused to look up at the building.

"It looks like some kind of fancy New England prep school," Naya observed.

It did. The rolling lawns, the elaborate landscaping, and the gracious, if imposing, brick structure combined to create a feeling of understated elegance and old money. If it hadn't been for the discreet brass sign that read 'Golden Village Assisted Living Center,' Sasha would have assumed the building was a private mansion and walked right past it.

She and Naya skirted the parking lot and circled around to the front of the building. Stairs led to a wide, shaded porch that was dotted with cushioned seating arrangements. Not one of the chairs or gliders was occupied.

They stopped in front of the leaded glass doors and smoothed their jackets and hair into place.

"Ready?" Sasha asked, her finger hovering an inch away from the doorbell.

"Let's do it," Naya answered.

Before they'd finished announcing themselves to the receptionist, Athena Ray, the administrative director of Golden Village, materialized to whisk them along a gleaming hallway.

"Please, sit." She ushered them into her office and gestured toward an old-fashioned couch with scrolled legs, a curved back, and a tapestry-like pattern. "Can I offer you a drink? Tea? Water? Coffee?"

"Nothing for me, thanks," Sasha said as she lowered herself onto the couch and looked around the office. It was stuffed with antiques—gilded picture frames, blue-and-white ceramic vases, even a bronze statue of a boy and a horse in the corner behind the executive desk.

"I'm fine, too," Naya added.

The director blinked at them from behind her oversized glasses and arranged herself in a Queen Anne chair across from the couch. "Well, do let me know if you change your mind," she said with a wide smile.

Sasha smiled back at her. "Thanks for agreeing to talk with us, Ms. Ray—"

"Please, call me Athena. And it's my pleasure. We take our guests' concerns very seriously. So if there's an issue with any of the research studies we participate in, I certainly want to know."

Naya cocked her head. "Your guests?"

Athena nodded. "Yes, guests. The residents who live in the independent apartments are called, well, residents, but we refer to those who move into our assisted living and nursing care units as guests. Patients sounds so clinical and unpleasant. In any case, I understood from Ms. McCandless-Connelly that there's some issue as to whether certain guests in our dementia care unit had consented to research that was performed on them posthumously. Do I have that right?"

Sasha nodded. "You do. Although I believe the, uh, guests in question signed up to participate in Dr. Allstrom's study when they were living independently—either as residents or possibly before they moved into the facility."

"Center," the director corrected her.

"Pardon?"

"We don't refer to Golden Village as a 'facility.' That sounds so cold, doesn't it?"

Sasha bit her tongue. She didn't want to spend her entire morning playing semantic games with this woman, so she just nodded and ignored the quiet muttering of Naya beside her. "Center, then."

Athena beamed her approval as if she were an elementary school teacher and Sasha a diligent, if not very bright, student. "Very good. Now, did you say Dr. Allstrom's running the study that Dr. Kayser is concerned about?"

"That's right."

"Well, I can assure you that Greta Allstrom is one of the most well-regarded genetic researchers in the city, perhaps the country. I'm certain that she wouldn't allow anyone on her team to cut corners, particularly not with regard to consent procedures." The woman's matronly teacher persona evaporated and she transformed into the consummate bureaucrat. She pitched forward, leaning in toward the couch. "As you no doubt know, grant funding is tied to compliance with federal regulations. Dr. Allstrom would *never* do anything to jeopardize her funding."

Sasha felt her eyebrow arching toward her hairline and smoothed her expression. Interesting that the faux-personalized luxury resort schtick went out the window so quickly. Forget about any ethical responsibility to the *guests*, the researchers were worried about their *funding*.

Beside her, Naya shifted on the couch, as if she, too, were uncomfortable with the woman's sudden change in demeanor.

Sasha held up a hand, palm facing the administrator. "Be that as it may, Athena, Dr. Kayser knows of at least four pat—er, guests—who enrolled in Dr. Allstrom's study and consented to regular blood draws but who did not consent to donate brain tissue after their deaths. All four individuals were housed in Golden Village's dementia care unit when they passed away. All four individuals were autopsied; in all four cases, brain tissue was removed and forwarded to Dr. Allstrom. And before you ask, no, in none of the cases was the next of kin either asked or informed about the brain tissue removal." She nestled herself against the back of the couch and waited.

Athena blinked rapidly and the color drained from her face. She shook her head. "That's not possible."

"And yet, here we are," Sasha responded. Naya coughed into her fist to cover a laugh.

"No. This can't be right." The woman seemed to be speaking more to herself than to Sasha and Naya.

She continued shaking her head as she stood and walked over to her desk to pick up the telephone. "Charles, is Dr. Allstrom in the building this morning?" she asked. After a pause, she said, "Yes, please. Tell her it's urgent." She replaced the receiver and looked over at Sasha. "Dr. Allstrom happens to be here today. I'm sure she can clear up this misunderstanding."

It seemed to Sasha that the woman was anything but sure, but she just smiled back at her. "Great."

Athena returned to her conversation area, and the three of them sat in awkward silence for several minutes. Sasha glanced down at her watch and then surveyed the oil paintings on the walls.

Finally, Naya cleared her throat. "How many people live here?" she asked.

Athena brightened, obviously relieved to be back on familiar footing. "We have forty individuals living in one-bedroom apartments and seven married couples, who live in suites in the carriage houses. Collectively, we call those residences the cottages. Our stepped-up care unit is housed in this building and serves up to thirty guests at any given time. The dementia care unit is also in the building. At the moment, I believe we have eight guests in that unit, although there are twelve beds."

"The apartments and carriage houses are on the grounds, too?" Sasha asked. She craned her neck toward the window. She hadn't spotted any other structures, but the property looked like it extended as far she could see.

"Yes. We own three acres, which, as you can appreciate, is quite an expansive footprint for an urban location."

"Three *acres?*" Naya repeated as if she must have misheard.

"Yes," Athena said, an unmistakable note of pride in her voice. "We own the entire block. The original property contained this main house, separate servants' quarters, and two carriage houses. In between, there are magnificent English gardens. We restored the buildings, taking care to keep period-appropriate touches, and then renovated the buildings to serve our residents' and guests' unique needs. Golden Village prides itself on blending modern medical technology with elegant, old-world charm." She finished her spiel with an expansive gesture toward the window.

Naya raised her eyebrows and asked, "So what's that cost for your guests and residents? I mean, ballpark."

"Costs vary depending on the individual's situation, but we view aging in place in comfort and dignity as an investment in oneself."

In other words, if you have to ask, you can't afford it.

Sasha was about to ask about the staff-to-resident ratio when a muffled knock sounded on the office door.

"Ah, that'll be Dr. Allstrom," Athena said as she practically ran to the open door.

~ ~ ~ ~ ~ ~ ~ ~ ~ ~

Greta couldn't imagine why she'd been summoned to Athena Ray's office, but then again, she wasn't overly concerned. Her relationship with the director of Golden Village was good, had always been good. In part, because Athena was more of a cruise director than a penny-pinching facilities manager. Her focus was on the residents' comfort and happiness and not on whether the research teams used too many paper towels or remembered to turn off the lights when they left a patient's room—which made Athena an anomaly in Greta's experience.

Her researchers were always glad to be assigned to Golden Village, and not simply because it was so close to the university. Golden Village was a genuinely pleasant place. Greta wouldn't mind ending up here herself when the time came.

So she was unprepared for what she found when the door to Athena's office swung open, and the director hustled her inside.

Athena was disheveled and slightly out of breath. The only way to describe her glassy-eyed expression was as one of terror. "Oh, I'm so glad you're here," she said. The words poured from her mouth in a rush, and she gripped Greta's upper arm hard with her bony, be-ringed fingers.

"Are you okay?" she asked, genuinely concerned by Athena's demeanor.

As Athena searched for an answer, Greta's eyes drifted over Athena's shoulder. Two women in business attire were sitting on Athena's Victorian couch, leather attaché cases at their feet. The African-American woman had short hair, styled back and away from her face to show off high cheekbones and clear skin. She wore a crisply tailored pantsuit with a lavender-colored collared shirt. The white woman was tiny, almost elfin, with wavy dark hair twisted into a high knot and pinned back. She wore a pink sheath dress with black piping and a long pink suit jacket. She was also wearing a pair of impossibly high stilettos—soft black leather, with pink stitching.

Greta sucked in a big whoosh of air. *Lawyers.* They may as well have been wearing flashing 'Esquire' signs around their necks. Under ordinary circumstances, she would have toed the university line and immediately called the legal department to ask for representation. Then she would have kept her mouth firmly shut until someone with a legal degree and bar admission card showed up to speak on her behalf.

But these weren't ordinary circumstances. She answered to two masters, and she was certain the Alpha Fund would not be amused to hear about legal machinations slowing down her work. It was better to see what these women wanted and figure out a way around it. Pronto.

Her eyes flew back to Athena's face. "What's going on?"

"These ladies have some questions about your research, Dr. Allstrom. Please, come sit." Athena seemed to get herself back under control. At least her broad smile was back. And her voice was the usual mix of soothing and lilting.

Greta followed Athena across the office, while the lawyers stood to greet her. Although Greta figured the black one for the senior of the two, the small, white one stepped forward first.

"Dr. Allstrom, it's nice to meet you. I'm Sasha McCandless-Connelly, and this is my associate, Naya Andrews." The McCandless-Connelly woman gripped her hand in a surprisingly strong shake, which caught Greta slightly off-guard. She took a closer look at the small woman and noticed that she wasn't delicate, just sinewy. Scrappy, even.

"Ms. McCandless-Connelly," she replied in greeting before turning to the taller woman.

"Ms. Andrews," she said.

"Pleased to meet you, doctor," Naya Andrews replied, extending her hand for another firm handshake.

With the formalities taken care of, Greta turned back to Athena, who was hovering at the edge of the Persian rug. "So, what's this about exactly?"

Athena's hand fluttered nervously toward her neck, but she caught herself and lowered it. "Ms. McCandless-Connelly and Ms. Andrews are attorneys."

"You don't say," Greta deadpanned.

"Yes. They're here because Dr. Kayser has raised some concerns about our, well, *your*, informed consent procedures."

Greta blinked. "What kind of concerns?"

"Why don't we all sit down? I'm sure Ms. McCandless-Connelly can explain it better than I."

The lawyers returned to their spots on the sofa, and Greta took the nearer of the two chairs. Athena sat down in the other.

"I'd be happy to catch you up on our conversation with Athena," the little one said. "But, feel free to call me Sasha. McCandless-Connelly's a mouthful, I know." She gave a little laugh.

Greta smiled politely.

The lawyer continued. "As we were explaining to Athena, Dr. Kayser contacted us on behalf of several of his patients and their families." She paused. "Do you know Dr. Kayser?"

"I know of him. We've crossed paths here, and elsewhere. But he's a clinician, and I'm a researcher. So we haven't had much occasion to interact."

The attorneys nodded in unison, and Sasha scribbled a note on her legal pad. Greta tried not to let the fact that her words were being recorded throw her off-balance. Despite Athena's evident case of nerves, she knew she had nothing to worry about. Her research protocols always complied with the letter of the relevant regulations. *Always.*

"You may or may not know that Dr. Kayser is a strong proponent of your research—well, all research—into aging-related dementia and cognitive impairments. He actively encourages his patients to enroll in studies like yours."

She didn't know that tidbit, but she was glad to hear it. "Good. We need more doctors like him if we want to eradicate dementia."

Naya jerked her head back sharply, as if some unseen hand had pulled her hair. "Eradicate dementia? That's a pretty impossible goal, wouldn't you say?"

"I wouldn't say that at all. My team is very close to unveiling a drug delivery system that would enable the human brain to repair itself," Greta told her in a matter-of-fact voice.

The two women sitting across from her exchanged skeptical looks. Greta hardly noticed. She was accustomed to naysayers doubting her. But Athena reacted.

"It's true. There's a team working on nano-robots right now," she enthused.

"Nano-robots?" Sasha echoed.

"Yes. However, I really can't get into the details just yet. I'm sure you understand. And, I don't mean to seem rude, but I am quite busy. Could you just tell me what precisely is troubling Dr. Kayser, so I can put your minds to rest and get back to my work?"

The request had the desired effect. Sasha was visibly chastened.

"Oh, of course. I'm sorry. Multiple patients who were enrolled in your study were given information about your research and signed consent forms agreeing to provide regular blood samples."

"Ah, yes. The informed consent materials were reviewed by the IRB at the outset of the study and deemed sufficient. And?"

"And, as you are no doubt aware, you never asked for permission to harvest their brain tissue, but you did it anyway." Sasha settled back against the couch and gave her a look that said, 'let's see you weasel your way out of this one.'

A wave of relief washed over Greta. If that was the extent of Kayser's concern, she could explain it easily. She took her time forming her answer, though, because she wanted to make sure the two lawyers would get the clear message that they were on a wild goose chase and back off. She couldn't afford to be distracted with legal wrangling, not at this critical point in the project.

"I assume you familiarized yourself with the Common Rule that the Department of Health and Human Services promulgated?"

Sasha answered instantly. "I have. DHHS requires that researchers obtain informed consent for federally funded research that involves the collection of data from living people with whom the researcher interacts directly. I'm paraphrasing, of course, but that's the gist."

"Right. And you said it yourself. Consent is required from *living* people. The Common Rule doesn't apply to tissue obtained postmortem. You don't think I took brain tissue from living people, do you?" She laughed at the notion.

Naya cocked her head and narrowed her eyes. Sasha sat up straighter and stiffened her spine.

"No," the senior lawyer said, "I trust you waited until they died. But you can't seriously be claiming an exception to the Common Rule because you enrolled living participants in a study, obtained specific consent, and then just waited for them to die. You could and should have obtained consent for the brain tissue study before they died. You had a duty to do that unless your IRB waived follow-up consent. Did it?"

Greta exhaled loudly. "That so-called duty is a gray area, at best."

"Did the IRB waive follow-up consent?" Sasha pressed.

"No."

"And you knew who the study participants were, right? I mean, you had research assistants coming into their rooms to draw blood on a regular basis. Why not just send them in with an explanation of the brain tissue study and a new consent form? Was it because you thought they'd opt out?"

She saw the trap a mile away. If she said yes, she believed the patients would decline to participate, she was admitting the research was improper. If she said no, she believed they would have gladly participated, then why hadn't she simply obtained consent? It was one of those lawyer trick questions she always saw on television.

"You mean 'when did I quit beating my wife'? The simple truth is that trying to obtain consent from dementia patients is a risky business. They may have had the capacity to consent at the outset, when they agreed to the blood draws, but once a patient finds himself or herself on a locked dementia ward—well, Athena can tell you, that patient is unlikely to recognize family members or know what year it is, let alone consent to participate in a research study."

"And you think that's a justification to disregard their autonomy?"

"No, that's not what I said. I stand behind my work. The Common Rule doesn't require me to obtain consent from deceased people—it's as simple as that. And I really don't have time to argue about it with you. My work is time-sensitive and, frankly, too important to allow myself to get mired down in complying with unnecessary regulations. I complied with the requisite rules. My IRB hasn't said otherwise." She stood and turned to Athena. "Now, if you'll excuse me, I have work to do."

11.

LEO THANKED HIS MOTHER-IN-LAW and tried to steer her out the front door. She'd had her coat on for at least ten minutes, but she was doing a cooing version of the cha-cha. One step toward the door, two steps back for one last cuddle with Finn and Fiona, who were happy for the interruption to tummy time.

"Valentina," he began as she turned away from the door and crouched beside Finn to perform the universal peek-a-boo gesture.

She looked up at him with large green eyes so like her daughter's. "Oh, I'm so sorry, I'm sure you'd like to get on with your day. Silly Grandma." She eased to standing. "Anyway, Leo, call any time you need a hand. I just love spending time with the twins."

He considered her for a moment. Then he said, "Actually, I was just wondering if you'd like to stay and join us for dinner. Sasha should be home pretty soon."

Her entire face lit up, and she graced him with a smile that stretched from ear to ear. "Oh, Leo, I'd love to. Pat is over at Sean's helping him rewire his dining room chandelier. I was planning to zip by Panera and get some soup for myself."

"Not on my watch," he told her. He held out his arms, and she deposited her coat into them then kicked off her shoes and joined the babies on the floor.

He hung her coat and then headed to the kitchen to put the finishing touches on the meal. He'd roasted a large chicken in a pan with autumn vegetables, planning to have leftovers for his lunch for the rest of the week. There'd be more than enough for Valentina.

As he dressed the salad and set the table, his mobile phone vibrated in his pocket.

"Connelly," he said, balancing a stack of plates in his palm and sliding the phone between his shoulder and neck.

"It's Hank."

"What's going on?" He glanced at the time display on the oven. 5:45. Since adopting the six Bennett children, Hank rarely worked past four o'clock.

He did, however, make exceptions for national security emergencies. "Is something going down?"

"What? Oh, no. The kids are over at the neighbors on a scavenger hunt. I checked my messages and already had the results on that search we talked about, so I figured I'd give you a call while I can hear myself think."

"Already? That was fast."

Hank chuckled. "I may have put a rush on it. Anyhow, he's clean."

Leo knew better than to say Wynn's name on an unsecured line. "No flags?"

Hank huffed out a breath. "No flags. But it's a slim file. He's got a year of birth of 1948, but from birth until mid-1975, your guy was a ghost."

"Meaning?"

"For the first twenty-eight years of his life, he may as well not have existed. No school records, no driver's license, no draft registration. Nothing."

"You think he's a spook?"

"It crossed my mind. He could be one of us."

Leo pondered the possibility. If another federal agent had information about his father, why wouldn't he just go through official channels? Unless the information could cast a shadow on Leo and endanger his own standing. Even though he was a contractor now, he'd been a federal marshal for several years—this could be an effort to protect him.

Valentina poked her head into the kitchen. "Leo? Do you need any help in here?" She noticed the phone to his ear and mouthed 'sorry' before retreating to the living room.

He waited until he heard her resume her high-pitched stream of chatter directed at the twins then lowered his voice a notch and said, "You think it's safe to meet with this guy?"

Hank answered instantly, as though he'd been waiting for the question. "Ah, heck, Leo, I don't know. It's a risk. How big of one? No telling. All I can say, is this guy doesn't have a record or anything approaching a flag. He's allegedly a retired fisherman, apparently did well enough to buy that house in Maine with cash."

Cash home sales were yet another tell that suggested Wynn was, or at least had been, undercover at one point in his career.

"Hmm. Nothing on the prints?"

"Oh, we got some hits on the prints. All yours. Do you need a refresher?"

Leo ignored the jab. "Thanks for the intel."

"Don't mention it."

He knew Hank intended for his words to serve as a literal admonition. They'd both have some explaining to do if Hank's database queries traced back to Leo's personal life. The government tended to frown on using their resources for personal purposes.

"Understood." He eased the roasting pan out of the oven and rested it on the stovetop.

"Have a good night."

"You, too."

"And Leo?"

"Yeah?"

"If you go up to Maine to meet this guy, take a friend."

"Right." Leo had no plans to travel to Great Cranberry Island without his Glock.

12.

ASHA WAS TYPING UP THE notes she'd taken at Golden Village when she felt someone watching her. Naya stood in the doorway to her office balancing a stack of files in her arms. She wore an expression that said she was trying to figure out how to broach a touchy subject.

"What?"

"What what?" Naya responded.

"Come on, I know that look. What's on your mind?"

Sasha had an inkling that Naya might suggest it was time to hire an actual legal assistant instead of piling that work on top of her own associate workload. And Sasha tended to agree. But what Naya actually said was completely unexpected.

She cleared her throat. "I don't know Mac, just thinking about what Dr. Allstrom said. She has a point."

Sasha searched her memory. It was entirely possible that the self-righteous geneticist had a point. But if she'd made one, it had been obscured by her didactic delivery. "About—?" she finally prompted Naya.

"About the need to get a dementia drug to market as quickly as possible. You don't understand what something like that could mean to people." Her voice quavered.

Naya's mom. Of course.

It hadn't even dawned on her that visiting Golden Village would exact an emotional toll on Naya. "Naya, I'm so sorry. I didn't think. That had to have been hard to sit through." Sasha's cheeks burned with shame. Some friend she was. Naya had watched her mother deteriorate slowly over several years, her mind ravaged by Alzheimer's, caring for her around the clock until her death a few years back.

"Don't be sorry. You were doing your job, and so was I." Naya's eyes flashed a warning—sympathy wasn't what she was looking for.

Sasha closed her notebook and walked around the desk to join Naya at the door.

"Right, we were doing our jobs. But that doesn't mean we don't have feelings." She placed a light hand on Naya's shoulder, half expecting her to brush it off.

But she didn't. Instead, she took a long, shaky breath. "This isn't about my feelings. My mama's gone. But there are other families out there—families who would give anything to get their parents back."

"No doubt. But there are also families out there who feel betrayed that their parents' final wishes weren't considered or, worse, were disregarded. No one's saying Dr. Allstrom's research isn't important or necessary, because it is. She just needs to follow the rules." Sasha was careful to keep her voice even and devoid of emotion.

All the same, Caroline slowed her pace as she passed by on her way to the supply closet, as if she could tell trouble was brewing.

"The rules? You mean the rule that she has to ask dead people to consent to her using their tissue and blood samples? That's not even required by the letter of the law." Naya's narrow shoulders shook and her chin jutted forward.

Sasha took her time forming an answer. While she was still thinking, Caroline returned with her box of pens and paused behind Naya.

"This sounds like that Henrietta Lacks situation," the secretary remarked.

Naya and Sasha turned and looked at her.

"Who?" Sasha asked.

"Henrietta Lacks. She died of ovarian cancer years ago, but researchers used her cells to create the HeLa cell line without letting the family know. It really affected her children to know that pieces of her were just out there ... floating around. Some journalist wrote a bestseller about it." Caroline gave her head a small, sad shake. "My book club read it last month."

"I remember hearing about that," Naya said slowly. She chewed on her lower lip. "I understand what you two are saying, but this research Dr. Allstrom's doing could change people's lives."

"It's a slippery slope, though. The law requires informed consent for good reasons. You may be right that Dr. Allstrom's actions comply with the letter of the law, but they definitely violate the spirit of the law." Sasha paused and considered what she was about to say. "All that being said, if you feel like you can't work on this case, I'll understand."

Naya stiffened, and Caroline hurried away, out of the danger zone.

"I didn't ask to get off the case." Her tone was measured but her jaw was clenched.

"I know you didn't. I'm offering."

She shook her head. "I'm going to do my job to the best of my ability, but that doesn't mean I have to like it." She locked eyes with Sasha. "I think a lot of people could end up suffering needlessly if All-strom's work gets bogged down in red tape because of us."

Naya turned and walked away.

She'd said 'because of us,' but Sasha knew what she'd really meant was 'because of *you*.'

~ ~ ~ ~ ~ ~ ~ ~ ~ ~

Sasha eyed her husband over the top of her wineglass. Something was going on with him. He'd been jittering his right leg under the table since they'd sat down for dinner. And now he was squaring his utensils and plate so as to ensure his place setting was perfectly aligned. The last time she'd seen him this agitated was the night they'd met. That evening, she'd chalked his nerves up to the fact that they'd just found a dead body in a Dumpster, but he later told her it was because he thought she was cute. Leave it to Connelly to be unfazed by a corpse but rattled by a girl.

She turned her attention to her mother, who seemed to be oblivious to her son-in-law's nervousness. Whatever was on Connelly's mind, it was probably best left unsaid until her mom left.

"Thanks for watching Finn and Fiona today," she said.

Valentina waved a hand and glanced at the twins, who were sound asleep on their blanket on the floor. "They were dolls. It was easy—and fun."

Sasha gave her a knowing look. Taking care of twin two-month olds was sometimes fun, but it was never *easy*. "It looks like you wore them out."

Her mother covered a small yawn with her perfectly manicured hand. "They wore me out, too. In fact, I hate to eat and run, but I really should get going. Dad texted me that he was leaving Sean's a half an hour ago. If I leave him home alone too long, he'll eat his way through a container of ice cream."

She stood and pushed in her chair then folded her napkin into a tidy square and placed it on the table. "Thanks for the delicious meal, Leo."

He came around the table to hug her. "You're sure you can't stay for coffee and cookies? Your daughter'll make me eat fruit for dessert if you go. Stay. You'd be doing me a favor."

Valentina giggled and patted his arm. "Fruit's better for you anyway."

Sasha retrieved her mother's coat from the hall closet and met her at the door with it. "Have a good night, Mom," she said as she helped her into her coat.

Her mom leaned in and presented her cheek for a kiss. "You, too, sweetheart."

Sasha wrapped her sweater around her body, hugging it tight against the chill and watched from the porch as her mother got into her car. She waited until Valentina had pulled out and rounded the corner before going back into the warm house.

Connelly was in the kitchen, loading the dishwasher.

"I'll finish that," she said.

As she approached the counter, he blocked her with a playful hip check. "I'm done now." He added a dishwasher pod and started the machine.

"Just like a blister. I show up when the work's done," she smirked.

He shook his head and topped off her wine. "Here, finish off this bottle. Unless you want to join me for a scotch."

Uh-oh. Scotch. Either they were celebrating something or whatever he was nervous about was really bad.

"Wine's fine for me."

While he poured his drink, she checked on the babies; they were still sleeping. Finn had rolled to his side and thrown an arm around his sister. Her heart squeezed at the sight.

She joined Connelly in front of the fire and leaned in close. "So, what did you have to tell me?"

"Tell you?" he echoed.

She cocked her head. "Come on, Connelly. You don't think I can tell that there's something on your mind? You did everything but pull out a ruler to line up your silverware at dinner."

He chuckled and shook his glass gently, swirling the liquid inside around the lone ice cube. "Hank got back to me about my dad. Well, about Doug Wynn."

"And?"

"As far as he can tell, Wynn is clean."

"That reminds me," she said, "Naya wasn't able to find out anything about Mr. Wynn, but she did manage to figure out how *he* found *you*."

He looked up from the glass with an expression of mild surprise. "She did? How'd he track me down?"

"My mother."

"Pardon?"

She took a sip of wine. "Apparently, my mom announced the twin's arrival to her church. I think she sponsored altar flowers in their honor, if I remember correctly. Anyway, the church newsletter—which is available as a public PDF on the website archives—lists our address in case anyone wanted to send a gift or card or drop by with a dish."

He nodded slowly, and she knew he was remembering the outpouring of dinners, tiny, adorable outfits, and soft, handmade blankets from the parishioners of St. Mark's. "Honest mistake. But even if the bulletin or whatever it was listed our names, how'd this guy know that Leo Connelly is me? I mean, that I'm the kid of this guy he might know?" He shook his head at himself. "Do you follow?"

"How'd he know you're looking for your dad?"

"Right?"

"I'm not sure he did," she said, rocking back in the Amish-made rocker her parents had given her as a baby gift. "I think, assuming he does know your father, he would know your mom's name. And she had no reason to hide her whereabouts. Naya tells me it's pretty easy to find information about her online—including the fact that she had one son, Leonard."

He was staring into his glass again.

"Connelly?" she prompted when he didn't respond.

"Sorry. Yeah, that follows. I know she said she tried to get the news that she was pregnant back to my dad. When I was sixteen, she gave me his first name and the name of the village where he lived. That's all she had. I guess it's conceivable that he did learn about my conception." He gave a little laugh at his own play on words. "But why reach out to me now?"

She didn't have an answer for that. "I don't know. Why not now? What is his name, anyway?"

"Duc."

"Duc," she repeated. She rocked forward and stood. Then she walked over to Connelly's chair and perched on the arm. She rubbed his shoulders and then rested her hand on his forearm. "Are you going to go meet Wynn?"

He hesitated. "Yes."

"I'm coming with you."

"No."

"Yes, I am."

He grabbed her hand between his and stared hard at her face. "That's crazy. We don't know anything, really, about this guy or what he wants. And, what exactly do you intend to do with the twins?"

"Bring them."

"What? No. No, no, no."

"Yes."

"Sasha—"

She cut him off. "Listen. If you think I'm letting you do this alone, you're the crazy one. This guy could have good news about you father. Or he could have bad news. Or it could be a scam. Either way, though, we're in this together—for better or worse. I'm going to be there for you."

"You can't drag the babies to coastal Maine in late October—it might as well be the dead of winter up there."

"I'm fairly certain even coastal Maine has hotels—they're probably even heated."

"Great Cranberry Island? That sounds like a hopping tourist destination to you?"

She waved off the question. "I don't know. If there's no hotel, I'm sure we can rent a house from a private owner. Don't get mired in the details. Caroline can make the arrangements tomorrow. Hank will be happy to watch Mocha, and Naya can come over to feed Java while we're gone." She bounced a bit on the arm of the chair, buzzing with excitement at the prospect of a trip.

"I really don't think this is a good idea," he continued.

"Look. I've been more or less cocooning with Finn and Fiona for months. Don't get me wrong, it's cozy. But, I think a little getaway is exactly what I need. What *we* need. There's been a dearth of adventure in our lives."

He dragged his fingers through his thick, dark hair then gulped his drink. "No adventure," he said firmly.

"Fine. Activity. There's been a dearth of activity. I solemnly swear that while you're meeting with Wynn, the babies and I will be engaged in safe, non-adventurous tourist activities."

The faintest hint of a smile developed on his lips. "Such as?"

She thought for a moment, trying to come up with suitably staid-sounding options. "Such as browsing antique stores and touring museums. Maybe we'll go wild and check out a story time at a library or bookstore." She fixed him with her most dazzling smile and blinked innocently.

An actual laugh escaped from his throat. "It's pointless to fight you on this."

"It's pointless to fight me period, end of sentence," she corrected him.

He nodded wryly and then leaned in to cover her mouth with a kiss. "Amen to that."

Fiona whimpered in her sleep. Sasha rested her wineglass on the side table.

"I'm so glad you've seen the light." She rested her hands on his warm chest for a moment. "I'm going to take Fiona up to bed to feed and change her. Bring Finn up after you finish your drink?"

"Okay."

"I love you."

"I love you more," he responded.

She bent and gently moved Finn's arm then scooped up Fiona and headed for the staircase. As she mounted the first step, she thought she heard Connelly mutter something about, "Not what Hank meant when he said bring your friend."

She paused and turned. "I didn't catch that," she stage whispered, cradling Fiona against her chest.

"Nothing important. I'll be up in a few."

She held his gaze for a moment, but he didn't say anything further, so she continued up the stairs.

13.

GRETA SQUINTED AT THE TEST results on the monitor, searching for a pattern in the noise. The soft rap on her office door barely registered. After a moment's delay, she swiveled her chair toward the entrance and called, "Come in."

The door opened. Mikki Yotamora craned her neck and stuck her head into the opening and said apologetically, "Sorry to disturb you, Dr. Allstrom. Director Buxton called the lab and asked to speak to you and, well, none of us knew how to transfer the call." The graduate student gave a sheepish laugh.

Greta tried to hide her surprise at the news that the director of the Institutional Review Board was looking for her and searched her memory for the instructions for transferring a telephone call. "Thanks for coming to find me, Mikki. Place the caller on hold, hit star 7, dial my extension, hit the TRF button, wait for the tone, then hit the hold button again." As she recited the directions, she scribbled them on a post-it note. She handed it to the researcher. "Here, you might want to post this by the phone."

Mikki bobbed her head in thanks and snaked her arm into the small space to take the slip of paper. "Thanks, Dr. Allstrom." She pulled the door shut, and Greta could hear her quick footsteps as she hurried down the hallway back to the lab.

Greta used the delay to save her work and close the window on her computer so she wouldn't be distracted during the call. There could really be only one reason Virgil Buxton would be calling her: Golden Village and the visit from the blasted lawyers. She should have known it would get back to him. She closed her eyes and took a centering breath. Last semester, the university had sponsored a mindfulness seminar for the faculty. Although she'd pooh-poohed the notion at the time, she figured it couldn't hurt now. Any port in a storm and all.

The phone came to life on her desk. She opened her eyes and lifted the receiver. "Virgil?"

"Dr. Allstrom," he responded, all business, "I understand from your student that you're in the middle of something. I apologize for the interruption, but this is important."

"Of course." She was thrown slightly off-balance by his formal tone. Although Virgil Buxton wielded enormous power, he usually projected an affable, friendly persona. This bureaucratic version of Virgil did nothing to assuage her worry.

"I received a call from Athena Ray this morning."

She groaned inwardly. She'd thought she'd managed to smooth things over with Athena before she'd left Golden Village yesterday afternoon. Apparently, she'd thought wrong.

Virgil seemed to be waiting for her to say something. "Is this about Dr. Kayser's issue with my informed consent procedures?" she asked, knowing full well that it was. "I explained to his attorneys yesterday that—"

"What on earth did you think you were doing? Why would you meet with attorneys without someone from the legal department present, Greta?"

She winced at the stern tone and sigh of disappointment but allowed herself to feel a smidgeon of relief at the fact that at least he'd used her first name. "Virgil, it wasn't a planned meeting. I was checking on our subjects when Athena called and asked me to come by her office. I didn't even know the lawyers were there," she protested.

"All the same, this is a problem. You should have referred them to the university counsel's office."

"You're right. I'm sorry," she answered meekly. In point of fact, she wasn't sorry, not in the least. Trying to handle the situation herself was the right call. It was the most efficient, least disruptive option. Having a team of in-house lawyers crawling all over her lab and her records would waste time, prove distracting, and possibly set her behind in her timetable. It had *definitely* been worth trying to resolve the situation on her own. The memory of the Alpha Fund's stance on delays made her shiver. But now a setback seemed inevitable, unavoidable.

Virgil's tone softened slightly. "Apology accepted. I'm sure you were only trying to protect your project."

Or maybe not so unavoidable. Maybe she could convince Virgil to keep the legal folks at bay. "I was," she hurriedly assured him. "You may not know this, but we're at a truly critical juncture in the research. Any distraction from our work would be a huge detriment right now. I still should have followed protocol, of course, but I really didn't see the harm in explaining to the attorneys that Dr. Kayser's concerns are misplaced."

"Are they?"

"Are they misplaced?" she asked, seeking clarification.

"Yes."

"Of course they are. You reviewed my informed consent forms yourself. They comply with the DHHS regulations. To the letter."

"I pulled out my notes this morning after the call from Mrs. Ray. I stand behind the forms as far as they go, but according to the lawyers, your current research exceeds the scope of the consent. Is that true?"

She pinched the phone between her ear and shoulder and scrubbed her face with her hands before answering. "I would say no."

He sighed. "Go on."

"Dr. Kayser's patients—all of the study participants—were advised of the purpose of the study and what we'd be doing with their blood samples. They signed forms consenting to provide regular blood draws." She paused and searched the tile drop ceiling for inspiration as she considered how to phrase this next part. "Hypothetically, we either could have conducted a re-interview and gotten a new consent form or, at the outset, could have obtained a blanket consent to additional research. But neither option was practical in this case."

"Why not?"

"Well, at the outset, the study design didn't call for further research beyond the blood samples, so we didn't include a blanket waiver. Our results were more promising than even we'd expected, so the study evolved. It happens."

"It does. It happens all the time. And new informed consent to participate in the new research is generally preferable to a blanket consent, so I likely wouldn't have approved your original form had it contained a blanket consent. Which leaves the question—why didn't you go back to the participants and get new consents?"

"Two reasons. First, the participants are in varying stages of dementia, Virgil. Any consent they could have given would have been open to attack as not being truly informed."

He *hmmed* his agreement to that.

Heartened, she continued, "And second, the additional research requires the harvesting of brain tissue. That obviously occurs post-mortem. And, unless I'm mistaken, a non-living research subject is exempt from the informed consent requirements."

"Ahhhh." Virgil drew out the sound, and she could imagine the lightbulb click on over his head as understanding dawned.

She waited a moment for him to fully consider the situation then said, "So, we're good. Right?"

He waffled. "Technically, your program may be compliant." He hesitated and then said, "But it's a little too cute."

"Too cute?"

"Please understand, I don't believe you've done anything untoward—"

"Good. Because I haven't."

"However, surely you can understand that it looks a bit off. You enroll competent seniors into a study to draw their blood, wait until they're in full-blown dementia, add them to your brain tissue study, and then wait for them to die."

"That is assuredly *not* what I do," she protested.

"That's how it looks, Greta."

Her frustration level was rising, threatening to overflow and undo all the gains she'd just made with Virgil. She couldn't afford to let that happen—he was her lifeline to funding for the drug trials. Completion of the drug trials was her lifeline to the Alpha Fund's nano-robotics investment. And failure was out of the question. She forced herself to take a long, slow breath before she responded.

"I'm sorry to hear that it looks that way. I don't want to upset any patient families or clinicians—that's the last thing I want. But changing the project design now would be disastrous. All the work to this point would be for nothing. What can I do to ease your mind *and* keep the study on track?"

It was Virgil's turn to take a deep breath. She listened to his loud exhale and prayed he'd tell her to just stay the course.

He didn't.

"It's not my mind you need to ease, Greta. If I were you, I'd reach out to Dr. Kayser—not through his lawyers, mind you. Contact him directly and walk him through what you've just told me. You need to get him on board."

The ominous note in his voice wasn't lost on her. "Or else?"

"Or else, I'm afraid, I'll have to freeze your funding until you re-interview all of the patients and obtain new, expanded consent. I'm sorry, Greta."

"So am I." Sorry didn't begin to cover it. She was terrified.

"Don't concede defeat just yet. See if you can't persuade Dr. Kayser. You can be very convincing, you know."

A sliver of hope pushed through her dismay. *Convince Dr. Kayser.*

"Thanks. Virgil. I appreciate your candor. Now, if you'll forgive me, I really do need to get back to my work."

"Of course, of course."

She ended the call and stared blankly at the whiteboard that hung over her desk, not seeing her scribbled formulae, scrawled reminders, and notes about appointments.

Convince Kayser—one way or another.

~ ~ ~ ~ ~ ~ ~ ~ ~ ~

Doug reclined against the stack of pillows piled high in front of his headboard, which he'd carefully arranged just so to prop him up to a half-seated position, and sipped his lukewarm broth. After a moment, he noticed that the answering machine light was blinking. A red numeral 2 flashed on the display to let him know his answering machine had recorded two messages while he'd slept. He leaned over and pressed the play button.

"Mr. Wynn, this is Marie from Coastal Oncology Specialists, calling to remind you that you have an appointment tomorrow, October 20th, at eleven o'clock. If you can't keep this appointment, please call the office to reschedule."

Could it really already be October 19th? He pushed himself up onto his elbows and squinted at the date on his wristwatch. Yes, it really was. Just three more days and he would know if his son would stand by him. Three more days. He sunk back against the pillows.

"Doug? It's Stevey. My errand boy seems to have gone missing. I don't suppose you know where I might find him, eh?" Stevey's voice was wry and knowing. Doug shook his head. Apparently Stevey would never learn. If he knew—or even suspected—that his messenger was in a shallow grave, why on earth hint at it aloud, let alone on a recorded message that could theoretically be discoverable evidence some day.

Stevey's message continued:

"Oh. A friend of mine who works for the airlines gave me a head's up. Leonard Connelly booked a ticket on a flight to Portland. Actually, he booked two tickets. Anyway, it looks like he's headed your way. I hope it works out for you, old friend."

Doug's emotions cycled through excitement that his son was coming; irritation that Stevey had overstepped—he hadn't asked the man to monitor flights; anxiety about the fact that his son was apparently not coming alone; and, strangest of all, comfort from the genuine concern he detected in Stevey's voice. The news that Leonard was bringing someone with him resonated most strongly. Doug knew that his son had, at one time, been employed by the U.S. Marshal's Service. Although records showed him to be retired, Doug believed the maxim 'once law enforcement, always law enforcement.' A cold finger of uneasiness trailed along his lungs.

He considered calling Stevey to get more details about his son's traveling companion but decided against it. He didn't want to involve Stevey any more than necessary in his personal business. If the meeting with his son went poorly, the less Stevey knew, the better. No, the prudent course would be to prepare for his visit as completely as he could in the next three days. Two days, he corrected himself. Tomorrow would be taken up entirely by the long trip to the oncologist's office.

He gulped down the remainder of his soup, grimacing at the taste of the now-cold liquid. But he needed nourishment to keep his strength up. There was much to do before Leonard arrived. Much to do.

He swung his legs over the edge of the bed and pushed himself to standing. He was tough, he reminded himself. And unafraid—he added mentally—rolling up the sleeve of his pajama top and gazing for a moment at his faded tattoo.

14.

SASHA APPRAISED THE DIMINUTIVE WOMAN who struggled down the aisle, wrestling with her suitcase as she bumped against the seats that edge the narrow pathway. She was smaller than Sasha—which was rare in itself—but looked friendly, if harried. Late middle-aged, maybe older. So even if she didn't have children of her own, surely she'd been exposed to them in some capacity—as an aunt, a godmother, a neighbor? Please let her have the seat across the aisle, she willed silently.

Better her than the sour-looking businessman who interrupted his haranguing cell phone call long enough to roll his eyes at her as she juggled both babies while Connelly engaged in whatever top-secret machinations allowed him to conceal carry his weapon on a commercial flight. And definitely better her than the gaggle of bridesmaids and already tipsy bride-to-be who'd stumbled past on their way to the back, tiaras and sashes crookedly in place. Maine in late October seemed like an odd destination for a bachelorette party, but she wasn't one to judge.

She simply wanted to survive the plane trip with a minimum of nasty looks and muttered comments. It seemed that merely appearing in public with infant twins was enough to ruin some adults' days.

The woman stopped, checked her ticket, and scooted into the seat across the aisle from Sasha. *Yes*, Sasha celebrated silently. The woman tried in vain to hoist her suitcase above her shoulders to jam it into the overhead compartment. She rested it on the seat and then tried again. Another miss. Ah, the travails of the petite.

The woman's seat mate, a thin man in his twenties with a soul patch and a sketchbook lolled his head against the window, sleeping. He wasn't going to come to her aid. Sasha sensed the opportunity to buy some good will.

"Excuse me, ma'am?" she said.

The frazzled woman turned. "Yes?" Her eyes were enormous, magnified behind her glasses.

"If you'll hold my babies for a moment, I can get that up there for you." She nodded toward the suitcase.

"Oh ... I can call the flight attendant." She trailed off and looked at the stream of passengers making their way along the aisle. It would be quite some time before a flight attendant would reach her. In the meantime, Sasha was sitting right there.

"It's okay, they don't bite. No teeth," she assured the woman with a smile.

The woman gave a little laugh and held out her arms. "Thank you. That's very kind. I must warn you, though, it's been a long time since I've held a little one."

Sasha eased Fiona into the woman's open arms first. Fiona immediately curled a tiny fist around the woman's shoulder-length hair and gave it a tug. Then she placed Finn in the crook of the woman's free arm. He batted his eyelashes and cooed up at her as if he were taking stage directions. She hurriedly grabbed the suitcase and hefted it overhead. It landed with a thud in the compartment, and she retrieved the twins, gently prying Fiona's fingers off the woman's hair in the process.

"Thank you so much," the woman breathed. She held onto Finn a split-second longer than absolutely necessary, and Sasha concealed her smile.

Mission accomplished.

"It was my pleasure."

"Your babies are adorable," the woman re-marked as she settled into her seat and tightened her lap belt into place.

"Thank you."

"How old are they?"

"Ten weeks."

"Tiny things. Are you traveling alone with them?" She said in a conversational tone.

"No, my husband's around here somewhere. Probably in the cockpit making a nuisance of himself." She leaned across the aisle. "He's a retired Air Marshal."

"Oh? What does he do now?"

"He's a security consultant." And then, although the woman hadn't asked, she felt compelled to add, "I'm a lawyer."

"My, you must have your hands full. I was a teacher for years, but when I had *my* twins, I quit to stay home with them."

"You have twins, too?"

The woman smiled at some memory. "Oh, yes. I'm on my way to Maine to visit my Roland, as a matter of fact. He's an artist. His sister Rebecca is a mechanical engineer." She smiled at some private memory. "Once they were in high school, I went back to work."

"Teaching?"

"No, journalism, actually. I'd written some articles for parenting magazines over the years. I started out covering the education beat and moved on from there. When I retired, I'd been the crime reporter for almost a decade. Now I write the occasional freelance article when something moves me. My name's Annabeth Douglas, by the way." She extended her hand across the aisle. She had a firm, businesslike handshake.

"Sasha McCandless-Connelly. This is Finn. And this is Fiona," Sasha said in return, pointing to each twin's head in turn.

From there, their conversation flowed naturally, as if they'd known each other for years. At some point, Connelly returned and settled into the window seat. Sasha introduced him to Annabeth and handed off Finn, who was fast asleep before the plane's wheels retracted.

Connelly nestled his son into his chest and peered through the window, staring out at the clouds. Annabeth pulled out a book, and Sasha played a quiet game of patty-cake with Fiona.

Fiona squealed with laughter, and Connelly turned to smile at her.

"What are you thinking?" Sasha asked when she caught his eye.

His smile faded. "Hoping this wasn't a mistake."

"Which—meeting this guy or letting us tag along?"

"All of it." His lips curved into a smile. "I'm glad you're here, though."

"So am I. And the twins are being awesome."

"Don't jinx it," he warned. "We're not there yet. We still have to rent a car, drive for hours, take a water taxi, and then somehow navigate Great Cranberry Island on foot, with the terrific twosome in tow."

Sasha dismissed the litany with a wave of her hand, even though thinking of the journey ahead exhausted her.

Annabeth leaned over. "Did I hear you're headed to Great Cranberry Island?"

"That's right," Connelly answered.

"My husband and I spent a week there, ages ago, with friends. There's not really much to do, but there's a cute little general store with a cafe. Make sure you get some homemade cookies for energy. You'll be flagging by the time you get there." She nodded toward the babies. "That's quite a haul for the little ones."

"It is," Sasha agreed. "But we didn't want to send daddy up without us."

"So this is a business trip? It's not really the tourist season up there, now, I'm afraid."

"I know. I wouldn't say it's necessarily a business trip, but it's ... personal business. Leo's been trying to find his father. There's a gentleman on the island who may have some information for him. After they meet, we're going to spend a few days visiting Acadia, if the weather cooperates."

Connelly shot her a dark look, but she ignored it. The fact that he was searching for his father wasn't classified. She was just making conversation.

"Oh, how exciting!" Annabeth clapped her hands together. "Are you nervous?" she asked Connelly.

"No." He turned back to the window.

"Sorry," Sasha mouthed.

"No apologies necessary. Sometimes I forget I'm not a reporter any more. When I was working, it was my job to pry. Now it's just nebby." Annabeth laughed.

Connelly must have realized his behavior was rude, because he looked back at them with a sheepish expression. "It's just not a very interesting subject. I'd much rather hear about you. What was the most exciting crime you covered?"

As Annabeth began to prattle about a story involving a long-ago trial of a New York City gang, Sasha smiled to herself. Connelly had a talent for getting people to talk about themselves. For the first time, she wondered if he'd developed it, not—as she'd always assumed—as part of his secret agent man arsenal, but as a coping mechanism to avoid having to talk about his fatherless childhood.

~ ~ ~ ~ ~ ~ ~ ~ ~ ~

Sasha hauled Annabeth's suitcase down from the overhead compartment and handed it to her. "Have a nice visit with your son."

"Thanks, dear. Here, take my card." She pressed a business card into Sasha's hand. "If nothing else, send me an email some time. I'd love to hear how your trip went and maybe see some pictures of those two little pumpkins in their Halloween costumes."

"Oh. Oh, thank you." She dug around in her wallet for a business card of her own to exchange, but the woman was already halfway down the aisle.

"She was nice," Connelly said.

Sasha nodded her agreement and did a final sweep of their seats to confirm they weren't leaving a blankie, a board book, or—in Finn's signature move—one lone baby sock—behind.

"I think we have everything," she said, as she shrugged into one of the hiking backpacks they'd decided to use in place of traditional diaper bags on this trip and then strapped Finn into the front carrier slung over her chest.

Connelly put on the second backpack and then the second baby carrier. He maneuvered Fiona into the carrier and secured the straps. "All set?" he asked.

"All set."

They strode through the spotless, nearly empty airport terminal and followed the signs to the rental car counters. While Connelly acquired the car, Sasha headed for the family restroom. She re-diapered the twins and listened to her voicemails at the same time. A court reporter calling to confirm a deposition, a reminder about a bar committee meeting, and a request for a donation. No calls from courthouse clerks, panicked clients, or irate opposing attorneys. All in all, the best-case scenario.

Will had almost managed to hide his dismay at the news that his recently-returned-from-maternity-leave law partner was jetting off on an unscheduled trip on short notice. The least she could do to repay him for that kindness was to stay on top of her messages and emails.

Emails.

As she repacked the wipes into the backpack, she spotted her phone, its red light blinking to let her know that emails awaited. Her hand hovered over it and she began to pull it from the side pocket, but she knew the emails would far outnumber the voicemails. She didn't have time to start that little project in the restroom. She stowed the phone and pushed open the bathroom door with her hip.

Connelly was leaning against the tile wall, dangling the rental car keys from his hand. He reached out and relieved her of half of her baby load. She allowed herself a brief moment's satisfaction at the well-oiled McCandlesss-Connelly traveling machinery. Later, after the machinery broke down, she'd be grateful she'd kept her thoughts to herself, so Connelly couldn't accuse her of tempting fate.

15.

LEO SHIVERED IN HIS THIN jacket as the wind swept across the highway. He pawed through the backpack until he found the unopened package of baby wipes; then he closed the rental car's trunk with a slam and jogged around to the passenger side. Sasha was leaning over the front seat, zipping Finn into a clean sleeper.

"Found them," he announced.

She glanced over her shoulder. "Can you get started on the carseat? But give me a couple first. I'm all out, and I have vomit under my nails."

He almost laughed at the incongruity between the image and the words. With her arched back and over-the-shoulder expression and the breeze lifting her long, loose wavy hair, she could have been a model on an exotic shoot. But her request laid bare the reality: she was a traveling mom with a carsick infant.

He handed her a fistful of wipes, held his breath, and got to work wiping down the carseat. One seat over, on the other side of the back seat, Fiona giggled and gurgled, either oblivious to or amused by her brother's predicament.

"There." He tossed the used wipes into the ziplock bag that held Finn's soiled outfit and closed it.

Sasha lifted Finn and traded him for the bag. "Poor little guy. I hope he's feeling better now."

Leo buckled his son into the carseat and kissed his forehead while Sasha popped the trunk and stowed the bag.

Once they were back in the front seat, Leo checked his mirrors and prepared to merge off the shoulder and back onto the highway.

"Does the house you rented have a washer and dryer?" he asked, suddenly wondering what they were going to do about Finn's vomit-coated clothes.

"Are you new here? Of course it does. Who would plan a long weekend with two-month-old babies and no access to a washer and dryer?" She laughed at the question and then returned to examining her fingernails.

He nodded and then hit the gas, seamlessly rejoining the flow of traffic streaming north on Interstate 295. They drove in silence for several minutes, then Sasha unbuckled her seatbelt and twisted around to check on their two tiny passengers.

"How's everybody doing back there?"

"Finn's asleep, and Fiona's trying to see if she can get her foot into her mouth." She settled back into her seat, keeping her voice soft so as not to disturb the peace that had fallen over the car.

He was continually amazed by how quickly the mood could change with babies. Minutes ago, Finn was red-faced and howling. Now he was calmly sleeping. Sometimes one of the twins would go from alert curiosity to drowsy, heavy-lidded quiet in mere seconds.

"I hope Fiona naps, too. We still have a good two hours' of driving until we get to Mt. Desert Island." And then they'd have to get a boat to Great Cranberry Island. They had hours of traveling ahead of them.

Sasha responded by looking pointedly at her empty takeout coffee cup.

"Don't worry," he assured her. "We'll stop for a quick lunch. But we really should try to lay down some miles while the twins are cooperating. I really don't want to get to Great Cranberry Island too late."

She shrugged.

She wasn't worried. *He* was worried. They would likely arrive early enough to take one of the three regularly scheduled ferries to the island, but all three ferries stopped running before six p.m. That would leave him very little time to actually meet with Wynn. So he'd called around and arranged for a private water taxi to transport them to the island, wait for them, and then bring them back. The captain had been amenable, but he was loud and clear about his personal belief that making such a trip, after dark, in late October, was foolish. When Leo mentioned the babies, the captain amended his opinion to 'damned foolish.' Leo privately agreed.

He felt her eyes on his face and glanced at her. "What?"

"I know what you're thinking, Connelly."

"Tell me—what am I thinking?"

"You're thinking that you'd really like to drop me and the twins at the rental house and go to the island alone."

"That's a great idea. I'm glad you've finally come—"

"No. Listen to me. You aren't doing this alone."

"Sasha."

"They'll be fine. We'll be fine. You'll see."

He shook his head. "I have a bad feeling about this."

She was silent for a long moment. Then she sighed and spread her hands wide in a gesture of appeasement. "We'll hang out at the cafe that Annabeth told me about, okay? We won't tag along to Mr. Wynn's house."

He kept his eyes on the road ahead and hoped he was successful in hiding his surprise. He could count on the fingers of no hands the times his wife had suggested a compromise with him. Okay, that was a bit of an exaggeration, but only a bit. She was wildly independent and accustomed to being right—two traits that didn't lend themselves to easy negotiation.

"Really?" he asked, almost afraid to believe she meant it.

"Really."

The tension he'd been holding in his neck and shoulders drained away. "That would be a great idea. What made you change your mind?"

"I wanted to come with you to be a support, Connelly, not a weight. It doesn't take a genius to see that you're extra uptight—even for you. You're not dumping us on the mainland; I want to be close enough to help if you need me. But if you want to go alone to meet your mystery man, we'll keep our distance." Her voice turned into a whisper that he had to strain to hear. "Just make sure you take your cell phone. And your gun."

"Thank you." He reached over and covered her hand with his.

She traced a circle on his thumb with the pad of her pointer finger. "You're welcome." Then she eased her hand free and rifled through the back-pack at her feet. "Speaking of cell phones," she said, more to herself than to him, "I need to charge mine so I can tackle my emails after lunch. My battery died right before Finn lost his breakfast."

She plugged the device into the charger, leaned her head back against the headrest, and covered a yawn with the palm of her hand.

"You should take a nap," he suggested. "That stupid phone isn't the only thing that needs to re-charge, you know."

She smiled sleepily and closed her eyes. "Maybe I will. You know what they say—sleep while the babies are sleeping. Or eating their feet."

16.

AL KAYSER HURRIED DOWN THE hallway and caught his receptionist's eyes as he passed by the waiting room, half filled with patients. She gave her head a discrete shake, wordlessly answering his unasked question. *No calls*.

He frowned. It wasn't like Sasha to ignore her emails. In fact, he'd emailed her precisely because he thought it would result in a quicker response. But several hours had passed since he'd hit 'send' and she hadn't called. He wanted to get her input before he returned Dr. Allstrom's call, but he couldn't wait much longer. He was likely to run into her in person in a few hours when he visited his patients at Golden Village, and he knew she'd use the opportunity to press him for an answer.

He put the issue out of his mind as he knocked on the exam room door. "Mrs. Baughman? May I come in?" He raised his voice so that she would hear him even if she had once again left her hearing aid at home.

When he emerged from the exam room twenty-five minutes later, Lucy was loitering near the copy machine.

"Dr. Kayser, I was about to leave for my lunch break, but I wanted to tell you—"

"Ms. McCandless-Connelly called?"

"No. But Dr. Allstrom called again. I transferred her into your voicemail." She winced slightly as she delivered the bad news. "Sorry."

He stifled a sigh. "It's okay. Thanks, Lucy. Go take your break."

He stashed Mrs. Baughman's chart in the slot designated for completed appointments and slipped into his office. He sat down at his desk and gnawed on his pen cap as he tried to decide what to do next. He hated to be a bother, but it occurred to him that he had no idea if Sasha had gotten his email. She could be in court or in a deposition or doing whatever it was lawyers did all day.

With that thought, he picked up the receiver on his desk phone and dialed the law firm's main number.

"Good afternoon, you've reached McCandless and Volmer. How may I direct your call?" Carolina Masters asked in her smooth as silk voice.

"Hi, this is Al Kayser. I sent an email to Sasha this morning, but I haven't heard back. I was wondering if she's in today?"

After the briefest of pauses, the receptionist responded. "Oh, I'm so sorry to hear that she hasn't gotten back to you, Dr. Kayser. She's usually very good about returning emails quickly, but she is traveling today. She may not have seen it yet. Can someone else help you?"

"Is Naya in?"

"Yes, she is. I'll transfer you to her line now, Dr. Kayser."

"Thank you." He settled back in his chair and listened to the hold music.

Less than a minute later, the music cut off and Naya's voice was in his ear.

"Dr. Kayser, Caroline explained you have an email in to Sasha that she hasn't had a chance to answer," she said by way of greeting. "I haven't read your email to Sasha, but could you tell me what it concerns?" Her tone was brisk and business-like.

He had to imagine with her boss out of the office, the junior associate was hopping busy. "Well, the short version is Greta Allstrom has called me twice today. She wants me to meet with her so she can, and I quote, 'assuage my concerns about her research.' I didn't want to agree to talk to her without getting Sasha's input."

"Assuage your concerns," Naya echoed.

He nodded to himself as he answered. "Yes, that's what she said."

He could hear a faint tapping sound as she thought, as if she were rapping her pen against her desk.

"Hmm … I would ordinarily say there's no harm in hearing what the other side has to say. But this matter is so unusual, I don't know if that's the right course here."

"Unusual in what way—if you don't mind my asking?"

"I know you're looking into this on behalf of your patients and their families, and Sasha's convinced that Dr. Allstrom's behavior is improper, but you have to bear in mind that we don't actually have a live case yet. By which I mean, nothing's been filed in court, no official demand's been made of either the doctor or the university. Part of the reason for that is we don't actually have a client."

He could tell she was choosing her words with care, but it wasn't clear what she was driving at. He took a stab, "Do you need me to sign a retainer agreement? I promise I'll pay the fees, and I—"

She rushed to disabuse him of that idea. "No, no, this isn't about money. It's about the fact that we need a plaintiff who's suffered the harm. You're concerned about your patients, but you weren't directly impacted when their brain tissue was taken without permission. In other words, you don't have legal standing to bring a case in your own name— at least not civilly. You could report the violation to the appropriate oversight boards, but I know that would be politically difficult for you. That's one of the reasons Sasha went to Golden Village first. She hoped she could convince Athena Ray to be the one to put the screws to Dr. Allstrom."

He mulled over this information. "I see what you're saying. And I know from Sasha's report that Athena Ray assuredly didn't put the screws to Dr. Allstrom, as you phrase it, but, based on her phone calls, someone has."

"The IRB?" Naya ventured.

He had no idea. "Possibly. I guess ... I could try to find out? Should I speak with her?"

Naya exhaled loudly. "I'm not sure. Let me try to get ahold of Sasha; she should be on the island by now."

"The island? Sounds very exotic."

"Hardly," she said, choking back laughter. "Sasha and Leo went traipsing off to coastal Maine in the dead of autumn and took the babies with them."

"Oh. You're quite right; that's the opposite of exotic. Maine is beautiful, but it can be downright chilly this time of year."

~ ~ ~ ~ ~ ~ ~ ~ ~ ~

Sasha crouched beside the blanket she'd spread out on the floor of the quaint, if drafty, cafe and put a hand to each of the baby's cheeks to check their skin temperatures. Somehow, despite the fact that she was still shivering from the raw, windy water taxi ride, both twins were toasty in their hooded outfits. Finn looked at her curiously and flashed her a toothless grin, while his sister swatted her hand away in irritation. She apparently didn't wish to be disturbed from whatever private game the two were playing with the soft fabric ball and wooden block Sasha had given them to inspect.

She laughed to herself at her infant daughter's fierceness and instantly regretted it because the action set her teeth chattering again. She cupped her hands around the yellow ceramic coffee mug in an effort to warm them. The feeling in her fingertips had nearly returned when her cell phone chirped.

She glanced at the display: *Naya Work* scrolled across the screen.

"Hi," she answered.

"Hi, yourself. How's Maine?"

"Cold. Beautiful, though."

Naya chuckled. "How'd the little ones do on the trip?"

"They were great on the plane. Finn barfed during the car ride, which made me *really* excited about the water taxi portion of the proceedings, but he hung in there. Fiona was fine."

"Did Leo meet that dude yet?"

"He's at Wynn's house now. The twins and I are cooling our heels at this little general store with a cafe down near the dock."

"You didn't go with him?" Surprise rang through Naya's voice.

"No. I could tell the thought of me and the twins tagging along was making him extra anxious, so I offered to stay here."

"Personal growth, Mac. Very nice."

"Ha ha. It turns out I *can* compromise. Who knew? So, what's up? I skimmed my emails but didn't see anything particularly urgent. Did Will get a verdict back in that bribery case?"

"No, the jury's still out. I'm actually calling about Dr. Kayser."

"Oh, right. He did send an email saying he wanted to ask me a question. My signal's been spotty. Do I need to call him or did you talk to him?"

"He called me to ask what I thought and I said I had to talk to you first."

Sasha bit down on her lower lip. She had plenty of experience managing junior associates from her time at Prescott & Talbott. But Naya wasn't a typical baby lawyer. She was a self-possessed, confident middle-aged woman accustomed to making decisions. After a moment, she said, "Why don't you tell me what he wants to know and what your instinct tells you?"

"Dr. Allstrom wants to meet with him."

"Why?"

"She says she wants to ease his mind about her research protocol. From the messages she's left him, he gets the sense that she wants to convince him that what she's doing is perfectly fine."

"Messages plural?"

"Yep. Two today. He's been putting off going over to Golden Village this afternoon because he knows she's going to ambush him there."

"Hard sell, huh? Seems like she doth protest too much," Sasha observed lightly. Given Naya's personal feelings about the research, she didn't want to stir up any emotion.

"Maybe. But is it okay for him to talk to her?"

She turned the question around. "What do you think?"

Naya answered slowly. "Ordinarily, I'd say yes, go hear what she has to say. At worst, we'll get a sneak peak at her defense. And the best case scenario is they could work out a compromise."

"And in this instance?"

"I don't know, Mac. I don't like it. Athena Ray clearly didn't want to get her hands dirty, so she's unlikely to be pressuring Allstrom. But Allstrom's insistence on talking to Dr. Kayser makes me think someone's applying pressure. And that's got to be either her IRB or ..."

"In-house counsel," Sasha finished for her.

"So, no, right?"

"Right. If the university legal department is involved—or even if it's just the Institutional Review Board, you *know* the lawyers aren't far behind—then they should have reached out to us. They know he's represented. I don't like it. Call Dr. Kayser and explain that if Allstrom contacts him again he should tell her to have university counsel call me."

"Okay, that's what I thought."

"You thought right." Sasha smiled to herself. Of course she did. Then her grin faded. "I'm sorry that it looks like we won't have a clean and easy fix to this, though."

Naya's voice was firm and clear when she answered. "That's not your fault. And I'm sorry about before. I was wrong."

"What changed your mind?"

"Caroline lent me that Henrietta Lacks book. I guess ... I guess it's more nuanced than I allowed."

If compromising with her husband represented personal growth for Sasha, acknowledging that she was wrong represented the same for Naya. But Sasha was smart enough not to comment on it. Instead she said, "I'd love to borrow the book when you're finished."

"Right. Sure. I know you have nothing but free time on your hands," Naya cracked.

Sasha started to laugh, but out of the corner of her eye she saw Fiona pulling herself along the blanket, trying to reach for what appeared to be a very old, undoubtedly fragile, large urn.

"Gotta go!" she shouted as she lunged forward to catch her daughter before she could destroy the item.

17.

LEO TURNED UP THE COLLAR of his jacket and jammed his hands into his pockets as he trudged up the long, gradual slope that led from the heart of what passed for the town on this island up to the secluded cliffside home of Doug Wynn. The ferry captain had warned him it would be a long walk.

For all his careful planning to get *to* Great Cranberry Island, he'd somehow failed to plan to get from the dock to Wynn's house. If he were being honest with himself, he'd admit that he'd more or less assumed the man would have a messenger stationed at the dock on the appointed day, maybe holding a sign that read "Leonard Connelly," ready to whisk Leo to the meeting.

But when Eli Nicholas, the water taxi captain, moored the boat and helped Sasha step up onto the rotting wooden stairs that led up from the dock to the hillside, Leo had taken a moment to scan the arrival area. No driver awaited them. To be accurate, no humans of any stripe awaited them. When he mounted the stairs, he noted three late model cars in varying degrees of disrepair and a well-kept, plank-sided outhouse. Further up the hill, he spotted the cafe/general store that Annabeth had mentioned.

He turned back to Nicholas. "I don't suppose there's a cab service on this island?"

The captain looked back at him with an amused expression. "Don't suppose there is," he agreed. He tugged his hat down over his craggy brow and jerked his chin toward the store. "Ya might ask inside if anyone'll drive ya where you're headed, but they ain't likely to have any baby seats."

"The twins and their mother aren't coming with me. They're going to wait inside the cafe."

"Now that we're here, ya mind telling me what brings ya to the island this time of year? It ain't exactly a hot spot."

Leo hesitated. He'd made it a point to be circumspect with Nicholas. Given that he knew precious little about the man he was going to meet—and even less about the denizens of what he imagined to be a tight-knit island community, he hadn't shared any details of his trip with Eli Nicholas. All the man knew was that he was to ferry Leo and his family from Mt. Desert Island to Great Cranberry Island, wait until they were ready to leave, and then ferry them back. At this point, though, he didn't have much to lose.

"I have a meeting with a Mr. Wynn. He asked me to come to his home, but it doesn't appear that he's providing transportation," he finally said.

Before Nicholas could answer, Sasha stepped between them, a baby in each arm. "Listen, sorry to interrupt, but these guys are cold and cranky. I'm going in to the store. Good luck with your ... meeting." She stretched up onto her toes, and he planted a kiss near her upper lip. Then he kissed Finn and Fiona in turn and waved goodbye to them as she walked off.

After she'd disappeared into the storefront, Nicholas cleared his throat. "Ay-yup. Doug Wynn. He's not the type to send the welcome wagon. He keeps to himself mostly." He scanned the row of vehicles. "You're probably out of luck on the ride, too. I recognize these cars—they belong to folks who commute to work on the mainland. Although more likely than not, they left the keys under the floor mat." He chuckled.

Great.

Leo reached into his pocket and retrieved the slip of paper with Wynn's address printed on it. By now, the sheet was nearly ripping along the well-worn fold lines. "In that case can you tell me how to get to—"

"The Blue House," Nicholas finished for him. "Mr. Wynn may be a bit of a recluse, even for the island, but everybody knows The Blue House."

Leo waited.

"Head straight up the hill—all the way up the hill. At the summit, it'll branch off into two roads—one paved road that bends away from the coast and a gravel road that follows the curve of the coast. You want the gravel one. You'll pass five, maybe six, big old mansions—the rich people call them 'cottages,' but don't be fooled. Then it'll look like the houses end. Nothin' but dense trees for about a quarter of mile. Then you'll see a narrow path cut through the trees, just big enough for a car to pass. That's Wynn's driveway."

And with that, Nicholas had headed to the island's lone bar to wait for Leo's call saying they were ready to return to Mt. Desert Island. Leo could only hope the man would spend his time swapping stories and not downing pints.

He crested the hill with some relief and veered left to take the gravel road, as instructed. He passed the time imagining who lived in the enormous cliffside cottages that lined the coast and drinking in the breathtaking view. From here, he could see Cadillac Mountain and the fireball of sun as it prepared to sink into the sea. He allowed himself to enjoy the majesty of the sight for a moment.

Then he reached for his phone and activated the flashlight app before continuing past the cottage and entering a stretch of the road that was edged with tall trees standing sentinel. The transformation from coastal cliff to forest was abrupt and complete. No light filtered through the canopy of leaves overhead. It was an excellent spot for an ambush. He put his free hand on his holster.

He covered the quarter mile quickly. When he reached the narrow path that Nicholas had mentioned, he expected it to be hard to find. And, ordinarily, it probably would have been. But evenly spaced light posts bordered the driveway, creating a well-lit path. And at the end of the driveway, Wynn's house was lit up like a beacon. Exterior flood lights beamed down from all corners.

Leo stopped.

It was reasonable to assume the man had turned the lights on because he was expecting him. This was the appointed day.

But it felt wrong.

A person who chose to live as a recluse simply wouldn't advertise his location this way. And the bright lights would leave anyone approaching from the driveway exposed and vulnerable. Doug Wynn could be standing in front of the house with a shotgun, and Leo would never see him. He, in turn, would be lit up as if on stage.

Strolling up that driveway was a sucker move.

He veered off the gravel road and stepped into the woods. His approach would be unseen, but unfortunately, it would not be silent. Dried leaves crunched underfoot with each step he took, and the cracking of dead branches and twigs echoed like gunshots in the quiet night as he thrashed his way toward the side of the house.

He reached a clearing and dimmed his flashlight as he raced across the empty space to the next copse of trees. He pressed himself against the trunk of a bare-branched oak tree and stared hard at the house. From this angle, the lights created a checkerboard of shadows, but he was fairly certain he saw no one lying in wait.

Of course, that's not to say he's not standing just inside, behind one of those thick curtains, weapon locked and loaded.

Leo felt a twinge of irritation. He should have arranged for some sort of backup. How had he let himself walk into a possible ambush like a dope? It violated his training, his world view, everything.

Because you were so eager for information about your dad that you let it blind you to the situation, he berated himself. *And it's a little late for the realization now, so let's get on with it.*

Despite the cold air, sweat beaded his upper lip. He flattened himself against the tree and removed his gun from the holster and checked that the safety was engaged. Then he held his breath and ran to the next patch of trees, the final cluster on the left side of the house.

Now all that separated him from the front door was about thirty yards of semi-manicured lawn. He pushed himself off the gnarled tree trunk and started his approach. He was about to step down onto a pile of lawn debris and decaying leaves when he froze, his foot in mid-air.

That's not right.

He stepped back toward the trees and lowered himself to a crouch. Then he craned his neck skyward and aimed the phone's light at the trees behind him. Elm, elm, oak. He shined it toward the ground. Right at the edge of the flood light's range, a pile of red maple leaves and pinecones joined acorns, elm and oak leaves, and sticks to form a blanket of material.

The leaves and detritus covering the ground hadn't simply fallen there from the trees overhead. It had been placed there. An innocuous leaf pile?

No. The materials had been strewn across the area, spread nearly flat to form a rectangle, not raked into a mound.

It's camouflage, he realized. *But what's it hiding? And its placement couldn't be a coincidence, located in the shadows outside the flood lights.*

He felt around on the ground behind him and grabbed the nearest branch then edged forward a few inches. He rocked forward on his toes and used the branch to sweep the debris away from the nearest edge of the rectangular shape. He beamed the light at what was hidden beneath. Not the grass that should have been there, but a woven mat. He reached out with one hand and yanked the corner of the mat, pulling it toward him. It was a standard door mat, made of rattan or possibly seagrass woven into a loose pattern. Someone had affixed clumps of grass and leaves to the surface so as to make it blend more naturally with the debris that topped it.

He set it aside and peered into the hole that the mat had covered, already knowing what he'd see.

A deep pit had been dug into the ground. The bottom was lined with row after row of thin sticks standing upright, their tops sharpened into points.

Doug Wynn had a punji trap in his backyard. A trap made even harder to see by its placement just outside the brilliant spotlights. Anyone approaching the house covertly would naturally choose the shadows. And with the lights having impaired that person's night vision, he would almost certainly stumble directly into the ambush.

Leo stared down at the wicked cluster of sticks. Then he narrowed his eyes and swept the yard. The pit was meant to ambush anyone who tried to sneak up on the house from the rear or, as he had, the side. Anyone approaching in the ordinary course wouldn't come within fifty feet of the trap. If he were a betting man, he lay odds that there was a similar pit on the far side of the house.

He returned the mat to its place covering the hole with careful, exaggerated movements and scattered the leaves back on top. A close inspection would reveal that the camouflage material had been disturbed, but Wynn would likely chalk it up to wind or wild animals.

He stood and considered his next move. Retreat, walk back to the dock, grab Sasha and the kids, and get the hell off this island? Or advance to a meeting with a paranoid, dangerous, recluse?

He tightened his grip on his weapon and crossed the lawn.

18.

GRETA'S NERVES JANGLED AS IF she'd had too much caffeine when, in fact, she'd had none. Her heart had been racing for more than twenty-four hours, ever since the call from Virgil. She'd been distractible, absent-minded, and irritable. After a night of fitful sleep, she'd steeled herself and called Dr. Kayser's office twenty minutes before his scheduled office hours began. And she'd called a second time. But he had failed to return either call, and it was clear from his receptionist's tone that she'd been instructed to put Greta off.

Ordinarily, Greta's social anxiety would have compelled her to retreat into silence in the face of such an obvious snub. But, in this particular instance, she couldn't afford to indulge her solitary leanings. If she couldn't get Dr. Kayser to back off she'd have to seriously consider contacting the Alpha Fund. And that horrifying thought made her stomach churn and her galloping heart pound even faster.

So she'd spent her afternoon pacing the halls at Golden Village and pretending not to notice the quizzical looks Athena shot her way every time their paths crossed. By five-thirty, her energy was flagging and she'd begun to suspect that Dr. Kayser was so committed to avoiding her that he was going to skip his patient visits. She was pulling out her phone to make one final, no-doubt futile call to his office, when the flash of a stiff, white doctor's coat fluttering behind its owner caught her eye.

She stowed the phone and scurried down the hall. "Dr. Kayser," she called as he disappeared around the corner.

She was about to break out into a full run and chase the man, when Troy, the graduate student tasked with taking today's blood samples, rounded the corner coming from the opposite direction.

"Dr. Allstrom," he said in an urgent tone as he skidded to a stop a few feet away from her.

She stifled a groan and turned her attention to Troy. Kayser had given her the slip, but at least she knew that he was in the building. He couldn't avoid her forever.

"Yes?"

He tried, but failed, to catch his breath. "It's Mrs. Chevitz. She's ... expiring."

Greta nearly snapped that the woman wasn't a carton of milk, but, after taking a closer look at Troy's gray face and wide eyes, she restrained herself.

"Adina Chevitz? Isn't Dr. Kayser her treating physician?" A plan to turn the situation to her advantage was forming in her mind even as she asked the question.

"Yes," he panted.

"He just headed the other way, we should go get him."

She started down the hallway but Troy grabbed her sleeve and yanked her back.

"Wait."

She stopped, and he continued. "He knows. Mrs. Ray knows, too. They're going to meet her children and husband in the lobby and bring them back to her room for the *Vidui*."

"The what?"

"It's like"—he paused and pursed his lips in thought for a moment—"it's kind of like the Jewish equivalent of last rites. It's the prayer you say before you die."

"Oh." Suddenly, the woman's impending death was something more substantial than an excuse to chase down Dr. Kayser. Greta felt as though her feet were rooted to the ground and a heavy backpack were dragging her shoulders down.

"Dr. Allstrom?" he asked uncertainly.

"Sorry. I'm fine. We should give them their privacy."

He tilted his head and gave her a curious look. "Well, sure. But, Dr. Allstrom … she's enrolled in the study, and she's not on the dementia ward. This is big. I mean, isn't it?"

The import of his words broke through the fog of anxiety that had fallen over her mind. "Yes! It is."

Relief and something akin to joy flooded her body. Mrs. Chevitz's unfortunate passing would deliver *exactly* what Greta needed. Adina Chevitz would be the first enrolled control patient to die without showing any signs of dementia. The comparison of her brain tissue with that taken from the most recent deceased dementia patients—both those who'd received the supplement and those who hadn't—would provide the last missing piece of information she needed for the nano-robot programmers. Her death was the answer to a prayer. Greta wouldn't miss her deadline, and she'd never have to know what fate the Alpha Fund had in store for her if she failed.

"How do we handle this? Should I wait until after they've completed their prayer to ask her if we can autopsy her brain?" Troy asked.

"She's in the research group. We don't need any additional consent." Greta said the words with a confidence she didn't feel.

"Are you sure? She's still competent. There's no harm." In contrast to her authoritative tone, his voice was hesitant, unsure.

The harm is she'll say no, Greta thought. She simply could not allow this opportunity to slip through her hands. It was unthinkable.

"I'll talk to Dr. Kayser," she said. His patient's impending death would be the perfect chance to convince him of the importance of the project. She'd make him see how close she was to a breakthrough.

Troy nodded his agreement. His relief was apparent on his face. For a moment, she wondered if Virgil had said something to her team about the informed consent issue. But she dismissed it immediately. If nothing else, Virgil *always* followed protocol. He would never discuss her project with her students.

She set her jaw. "Head back to the lab and get everything ready. I want to be able to rock and roll as soon as we get the green light," she told him.

Then she set off at a brisk pace in the direction of the lobby.

~ ~ ~ ~ ~ ~ ~ ~ ~ ~ ~

Al Kayser saw Dr. Allstrom approaching out of the corner of his eye and frowned. Surely she wasn't going to accost him *now*. Had she no sense of decency? He had his arm around the shoulder of Adina Chevitz's weeping daughter, who'd needed to leave her mother's room to gather herself after the prayer.

"Shhh, Ruth, shh," he soothed her. "Excuse me for a moment," he said in a near whisper.

Then he hurried down the hallway to confront Allstrom at a reasonable distance from the dying woman's room.

"Dr. Kayser," she said, holding up a hand as if she knew he was about to castigate her. "Please. Let me talk." She spoke quickly, excitedly.

He knitted his eyebrows together but nodded. "Make it quick, please. I have a patient to attend to."

"I know. I heard about Mrs. Chevitz. I'm sorry."

Although her tone reeked of insincerity, he decided to take her condolence at face value. "Thank you. If you know about Mrs. Chevitz's condition, then I'm sure you'll understand that this isn't the appropriate time to talk about your research. I need to be with the Chevitz family."

She glanced over his shoulder at Ruth, who was no longer wailing but was sniffling into her handkerchief. "Of course." She paused. "I wonder if I could speak to Mrs. Chevitz or, in the alternative, a member of the family. Mrs. Chevitz is one of my research participants and—"

An unfamiliar anger blazed in his chest. "Not now, Dr. Allstrom. Have some sensitivity."

She flinched as if he'd slapped her but persisted nonetheless. "Of course. Perhaps after Mrs. Chevitz is ... gone?"

Al counted to ten before answering her. "I admire your commitment to your work, Dr. Allstrom. Perhaps more than anyone, I can appreciate how important the fight against dementia truly is. That said, this simply isn't the time."

He crossed his arms and stared hard at her until she lowered her eyes.

"Of course," she mumbled. She started to walk away and then turned back. "Please convey my sympathies to the family."

"I will," he promised, softening just a bit in his views toward the researcher. "Now, if you'll excuse me."

He rejoined Ruth Chavitz to see whether she was ready to go back into the room. When he glanced up again, Dr. Allstrom was gone.

19.

LEO STOOD AT THE FRONT door of The Blue House, stowed his gun in its holster, and smoothed his jacket over the top. The house was, unsurprisingly, blue. Not a bright blue, by any means; rather it was a weathered and faded blue, the peeling paint showing the effects of time, saltwater, and wind. He took one final astonished look at the dense forest that surrounded the house, obscuring it from the road and shielding it from the water below. Anyone out on a tourist cruise who scanned the cliffs would almost certainly be unable to see the blue house in the woods.

He lifted the brass knocker and let it fall heavily against the door. As he waited for someone to answer the knock, he wondered again what—or who—Doug Wynn was hiding from up here. Despite having uncovered his host's trap, Leo was remarkably unconcerned. He was confident in his ability to draw his weapon faster than almost anyone he might encounter—*punji* pit or not.

After several minutes, he raised his hand to the knocker again but stopped when he heard rustling on the other side of the door. Then then rasp of rusted deadbolt scraping as it was unlocked. Finally, the door edged open and a thin, haggard man peered out at him.

"Leonard Connelly?" he creaked.

"Yes. Is Doug Wynn home?"

Leo assumed the man was a caretaker of some kind. He judged the man to be in his mid- to late-sixties. Vietnamese. And clearly unwell. He had the gray pallor and hunched, too-thin look of a man battling illness.

"Come in." The man opened the door wider and shuffled aside to let him pass. After Leo crossed the threshold, he closed the door and relocked the deadbolt with a tremoring hand. Then he faced Leo and appraised him slowly, from head to toe, before announcing. "I'm Doug Wynn. Thank you for coming."

Leo kept his expression neutral and regarded him closely. Despite his frail appearance, Doug Wynn had hard edges and cold eyes. He extended his hand. "I guess it's nice to meet you," he said cautiously.

His adrenaline was still running high from the discovery of the trap but he didn't sense that he was in any physical danger from Wynn. Even if the older man were armed, he was too slow and unsteady to get the drop on Leo. He allowed himself to relax incrementally.

The man shook his hand gingerly. "Come. Sit. I didn't see a car. You walked?"

"Yes."

He followed Wynn through a dimly lit corridor to a large sitting room to the right of the door. Two overstuffed chairs faced a dusty fireplace. On the other side of the room, a sofa and a coffee table faced the window. There was no television, but the walls were lined with bookshelves groaning under the weight of books. Hardbacks, paperbacks, all manner of books were piled on the shelves. Not standing in tidy rows, organized by size, but in haphazard collections, some piled horizontally, some doubled up in two rows. Leo lowered himself into the chair next to Wynn as he craned his neck and tried to make out some of the titles.

The older man watched him. "You like to read?"

Leo turned his attention back to his host. "I do. It looks like you do, too?"

"Ah, yes," Wynn said. He smiled. "I guess the apple doesn't fall far, eh?"

It took a long moment for Leo's brain to process the sentence and spit out its meaning. He sat back in the chair and eyed the man. "Excuse me?"

Wynn nodded. "I'm your father. My name is Duc Nguyen. I Americanized it when I came to this country."

Here it was. The scam. The shakedown.

"Oh, I see," Leo said, letting his skepticism drip from his voice.

Wynn rocked forward and braced his palms on his knees. "You don't believe me." It was a statement, not a question.

"That's right. I don't." Leo stood. His heart pounded, and he barely kept control of his seething anger. He'd allowed himself to be dragged all the way up here, had dragged his entire family up here, and had spent the past twenty minutes traipsing around a booby-trapped yard in the cold for what had turned out to be worse than a wild goose chase. "I don't know what your con is, Mr. Wynn. But I'm leaving."

"Leonard, *con trai.* Wait."

Con trai. Son. It was one of the handful of Vietnamese words Leo knew.

The summer he'd gone to Vietnam in search of his father, he'd practiced two sentences until he could say them flawlessly: 'I'm looking for a man named Duc. I'm his son.' He mumbled the phrases to himself under his breath.

"Yes. You came to the village. I was already living in New York then. But my cousins heard about your visit, long after you had left, and got word to me."

Leo narrowed his eyes. "Let's say you *are* my father. You sure took your time trying to find me. I went to Vietnam in 1985," he said dryly.

"That's true," Wynn conceded.

"So why now? Why did you come looking for me now?"

The older man thought for a long moment. He steepled his fingers as he formed his response.

Seeing him make the gesture hit Leo like a gut punch. From the time he was a small child, he would do that with his hands when he was deep in thought. His mother used to smile when she caught him at it and would say, wistfully, 'Just like your dad.' And, just like that, he believed the man. Doug Wynn, Duc Nguyen, whatever he called himself, was his father. He heard his breath coming fast and ragged and steadied it with some effort.

Oblivious to his reaction, his father nodded to himself. "I believe you deserve the truth, so I'll be honest with you. I never planned to contact you. But, as it turns out, I need a favor."

Leo blinked. "A favor?" he echoed.

"Yes. I have cancer, and I'm dying."

He paused, and Leo wondered what his father expected him to say. 'I'm sorry,' seemed both trite and disingenuous, so he said nothing.

After a brief moment, Wynn continued, "It's in my liver, and I'm too sick for more chemotherapy. The medications aren't working. The doctors say I have weeks, maybe a couple months at most. Unless ..."

"Unless what?"

"Unless I get a liver transplant. My tumors are too big for me to go on the transplant list for a cadaver liver." Wynn stared hard at Leo. "But if I don't get any sicker, I could qualify for a living donor transplant."

"Okay?"

"I need to find the donor, Leonard. Not them."

Leo sank back down into the chair. "You're not seriously asking me to give you my liver. Are you?"

"Just part of it," his father hurried to reassure him. "They take, you know, just a portion of it. The liver regenerates. So if the operation succeeds, after just a few months, you will have a whole, healthy liver, and I will have a whole, healthy liver. It's my only chance, Leonard."

"It's Leo. Of course, you'd know that if you'd ever bothered to have a relationship with me."

"Let me very clear. I don't want a relationship with you. I want part of your liver." His voice was hard and expectant.

Leo barked out a laugh. "Why exactly would I do this for a stranger?"

"I'm not a stranger. I'm your father." Wynn's spine stiffened.

"You don't want to have a relationship. Did you even know that I'm a father? I'm married, and we have twin infants. You're a grandfather." The muscle in Leo's right cheek began to twitch, a sure sign that he was in danger of losing his grip on his rising anger.

"Congratulations to you."

"But you don't even want to meet your grandchildren?"

Wynn sighed. "It's complicated. There are reasons—important reasons—why I can't be involved in your life, and you can't be involved in mine. But our culture would require a son to do this for his father. I know you're American, but I am hoping that somewhere inside you, there's a part of you that's Vietnamese enough that you will do what I ask. You must understand, though, that this will be a gift, and after the surgery we'll go back to living our separate lives."

Wynn finished speaking and searched his face.

Leo shook his head. If nothing else, he had to give his father credit for his ruthless honesty. "I don't know what you want me to say. This is a lot to take in."

Wynn coughed into his fist, a dry, hacking cough that rattled his chest and set off a round of trembling.

"Do you need a glass of water?" Leo asked, concerned despite himself.

"Please," his father croaked and pointed toward the back of the house.

Leo made his way to the kitchen, found a glass, and filled it with tap water. He returned to the sitting room and placed the glass on the table between the two chairs. Wynn lifted it to his lips and took a small, slow sip.

"Thank you," he said faintly.

Leo abandoned any plans he'd had to confront Wynn about the *punji* pit he'd found. The man was dying. Despite the callous attitude he displayed, Wynn was asking his son for help. Leo could tell that dynamic didn't sit easy with the man. He tamped down his own feelings and crouched in front of his father. "I need time to think. Give me a phone number where I can reach you. I'll call you after I've talked to my wife."

Wynn closed his eyes and seemed to gather strength. When he opened his eyes, he sat up straighter. After a moment, he rose and crossed the room to an old telephone stand that occupied the corner near the windows. He pulled open a drawer and pawed around until he located a pen and notepad. He scrawled a telephone number on the pad, then ripped the sheet off and held it out toward Leo. "Here."

Leo walked over and took the sheet from him. His father placed his dry, papery hand on Leo's arm. Leo looked down at the man's pale skin, almost translucent, the blue veins so prominent.

"Talk to your wife. Consult your conscience. Call a doctor if you want to know more about the risks to you. But don't take too long. I don't have much time." He released Leo's arm and turned both of his palms upward as if to say it's out of my hands.

Leo shoved the paper into his pocket. "I have to go."

"Wait," his father rasped. He reached into the drawer and removed a set of keys. "There's a car in the woodshed. Take it. Leave it at the dock. Someone will come for it later."

"Are you sure?"

"Yes, take it." He dropped the keys into Leo's palm.

"Okay. Thanks."

He pressed a smaller key, the type that would fit in a padlock, into Leo's palm. "Go out through the kitchen. You'll see the shed at the end of a stone path. Leave the padlock unlocked and put the key on the shelf inside the door. I'll lock it up later. I'd see you out, but I need to rest." He lowered himself carefully onto the sofa and closed his eyes.

Leo stared down for a long moment at the father he'd been longing for, off and on, for decades. The emotions running through his mind were a jumble of disbelief and joy, regret and confusion, sorrow and anger. He opened his mouth to say something in case this was the last time he saw the man but closed it quickly because he had no idea what to say.

He swallowed. The he walked to the kitchen and let himself out of the house. On the back porch, he stopped to text Sasha to let her know he'd meet her in about fifteen minutes. As he was stowing his phone in his pocket, he heard the unmistakable click of a lock tumbler sliding into place behind him. He turned, and the flutter of a curtain inside the kitchen window caught his eye.

He squared his shoulders and proceeded down the path.

20.

WYNN WATCHED HIS SON STRIDE away.
That went as well as it could have, he told
himself. Not only had he made his re-
quest, he'd managed to get the dead kid's car off his
property. If the authorities found the car in the
ferry parking lot, he'd have what the lawyers called
plausible deniability. He smiled at his own clever-
ness. The cancer might be eating away his strength
but his mind remained strong and clear.

Only Leonard could tie the vehicle to him, and
Wynn didn't intend to invite him back to the island
again. If all went as planned, the next—and last—
time he'd see Leonard would be in the hospital for
their transplant surgery.

Suddenly, Leonard stopped, three-quarters
down the path to the shed, but well short of the

door. His head swiveled to the copse of trees to the left of the path and he craned his neck forward, staring hard at something.

Wynn's heart rate ticked up a notch. *Had he noticed the disturbed earth? It wouldn't do for Leonard to discover the grave and the body it held. He'd have to kill him, and any hopes of recovery would die with him. Unless he could find a corrupt surgeon willing to do an off-the-books cadaver liver transplant,* he mused. He instantly rejected that idea as impractical. *Too bad; it would have resolved the issue of whether Leonard would agree to the organ donation.*

He followed Leonard's line of sight and realized he was staring at one of the well-hidden traps he'd dug just after moving into The Blue House. He'd been stronger and younger then, and had dug the pits without breaking a sweat. A far cry from his current state.

How could his son have spotted the trap, and what would happen if Leonard fell into it—would his liver be unusable if it were punctured by dozens of sharpened sticks? He'd researched Leonard's background after Tran had coughed up his name, and he knew his son had some experience as an air marshal. But he hardly expected a flying policeman who'd apparently quit under a cloud to have such a keen eye. He held his breath as he watched Leonard stare at the patch of earth near the stand of dense trees.

After a moment that seemed to stretch into eternity, Leonard continued along the path. Wynn exhaled.

As Leonard proceeded to the shed, Wynn felt an unfamiliar pang of regret. Perhaps if he'd had a different life, he'd be a different man. More like his son.

Eh, he brushed the thought away, as if it were a gnat. *Things hadn't been different. They were the way they were. No regrets,* he reminded himself. *No fear, not of death not of anything. B.T.K.*

He waited at the window until he saw Leonard ease the dirty Honda out of the shed and along the driveway to the right of the path. Once the car was out of sight, he let the curtain fall over the glass.

21.

SASHA STARED AT THE SIDE of her husband's head and willed him to look at her. He didn't take his eyes off the road ahead. She pondered her next move. He'd been nearly mute since he'd shown up at the dock driving a dusty Civic loaned to him by Wynn. The closest he'd come to answering any of her questions had been monosyllabic grunts and cautioning looks, which she assumed meant he didn't want to talk about his meeting in front of Captain Nicholas.

And that was fine. Understandable, even. So she'd spent the boat ride asking Eli Nicholas inane touristy questions and learning interesting facts like lobster traps, once thought to be inescapable, were in fact the equivalent of lobster revolving doors.

But once they were back on the mainland, situated in the rental car, with two sleeping babies in the backseat, she *had* expected some conversation. Instead, he was doing an excellent impersonation of a taciturn Mainer.

She hit the button to turn on the radio.

"What are you doing?" he asked without turning his head.

"Looking for a public radio station. Staring at the patch of gray hair over your ear isn't as scintillating as you might think it is."

A shadow of a smile flitted over his lips then evaporated instantly. "That's silver, not gray, thank you very much."

"He speaks!" she said in mock surprise.

He sighed, letting out a great *whoosh* of breath. "I don't what to talk about it, yet. Later." His flicked his eyes in her direction. "Okay?"

"Of course it's okay. But I can tell that whatever you and Doug Wynn talked about is bothering you. I'm here whenever you're ready to tell me." She squeezed his hand to let him know she meant it.

He lifted her hand to his mouth and kissed it. "I don't deserve you."

"You really don't," she agreed. He gave her another sidelong glance, and she laughed so hard her sides ached. "Just kidding, silver fox."

After a few moments, she spoke again. "I meant to ask you about the car Doug Wynn lent you to drive back to the ferry."

"What about it?"

"I'm sure it's just a coincidence, but somebody reported a black Honda missing. There was a flyer up in the café. Actually, two. Stolen—or as the flyer said—misplaced black Honda Civic. And a Chinese kid—well, a young guy—who's gone missing. He was last seen in Mt. Desert."

Connelly's cheek twitched. "Was there a picture of the guy?"

"Yeah. Tall, skinny Asian kid. Last seen wearing a leather jacket and jeans." She gave a wry laugh. "Not much to go on."

"Oh, it's plenty."

She turned and gave him a puzzled look, but he didn't elaborate.

They drove in silence for several miles before he blurted, "His name's Duc Nguyen."

She startled. "Who? The kid? I don't think that's what the poster said."

"Doug Wynn. His real name is Duc Nguyen."

She considered this piece of information. "Nguyen? Is that Vietnamese?"

"Yeah. He Americanized it when he came here."

"So, does he actually know your dad?" she asked, her excitement mounting.

"Something like that."

His dry tone didn't match the import of that face. "Something like that? What does that mean."

He negotiated a hairpin turn in the road before answering her. "He *is* my dad."

For a moment, she thought she misheard him. "Doug Wynn is your father?"

"Yes."

She waited for something more. A display of emotion, an explanation of how his long-lost father was going to fit into their lives going forward. Something. But Connelly had lapsed back into silence.

"I don't understand," she finally said. "Why didn't you bring him with you to meet us? Or why aren't we staying with him? What *happened* up there?"

"Well, one thing that happened is I found a *punji* pit in his backyard."

"A what?"

"*Punji* pit. The Viet Cong used them to ambush soldiers. They'd dig a pit and fill it with sharpened sticks, sometimes the points would be smeared with poison or excrement from wild animals. Then they'd cover the pit with leaves and grass and wait for some poor soul to stumble into the trap."

"Wait. What? His backyard was booby trapped? If you'd have fallen into it, you'd have been impaled." she asked, her stomach turning at the thought.

"Probably," he agreed.

After a moment's silence, she asked, "Your dad was with the Viet Cong?" She couldn't imagine how a United States Army nurse and a Viet Cong soldier would have struck up a romance.

He shook his head. "I don't think so. I think he really was just some farm kid. But, he would have known how to make a trap. Everyone living in the war zone would have been aware of them."

"Okay. So why's he have one in his freaking yard?"

"Security, I'm guessing."

"Security? What's wrong with an alarm system?"

"I don't know his story, Sasha. But I'm guessing he has the kind of enemies that aren't going to be put off by a Guardian Protection sign in the flowerbed."

"Good Lord."

"And unless I'm mistaken, your missing Asian guy is the messenger he sent to Pittsburgh."

She caught the tremor in his voice and knew that he was thinking the same thing she was: the kid was missing, and Connelly had just driven a stolen car to the dock, conveniently removing evidence of a possible crime from his father's property.

"What have we done by inviting this man into our lives?" She glanced back at the two car seats and realized she was shaking.

"Oh, don't worry. He doesn't want to be in our lives." He barked out a mirthless laugh.

"Now, I'm completely confused. What do you mean? He obviously wants a relationship with you. He went through the trouble of tracking you down."

"He was very clear about the fact that he doesn't want anything to do with us." He hit the turn signal and headed up the gravel driveway that led to the rental house.

"We'll if he doesn't want to be a part of your life, what does he want?"

Connelly pulled up to the charming front porch and brought the car to a stop. He twisted in his seat and looked into her eyes. "My liver."

22.

ROY ASSUMED HE'D BE THE first one into the laboratory, considering that the sun hadn't yet even begun to poke its face over the Downtown skyscrapers when he raised his identification badge to the card reader and waited for the click.

But when he eased open the door to the lab, Mikki looked up at him from a thick binder.

"Oh, hi," he said in surprise.

"Morning. What are you doing here so early?" she asked with a smile.

"I was just about to ask you the same thing."

She turned to face him full on, and he could see the excitement shining in her eyes. "Dr. Allstrom texted me. She said we're going to have a brain sample later today."

"She texted you?" he echoed. Confusion and disappointment warred with anger but he wouldn't take it out on Mikki. That wouldn't be fair.

Mikki cocked her head. "Yeah. Did she text you, too? I can handle it on my own. In fact, someone must have come in and prepped everything last night. All I need now is the brain slices."

His shoulders slumped forward. "That was me. I was at Golden Village when Mrs. Chevitz took a turn. Dr. Allstrom told me to come prep. I just assumed ..."

"I would have assumed it was my brain, too, under the circumstances," Mikki was quick to reassure him. "It's not like Dr. A to play favorites. I'm sure it was an oversight."

"I guess," he said, unable to keep the dismay out of his voice.

"Listen. You did all the grunt work. And you're here now. Let's just do the work up together."

He blinked and studied her closely. "Do you mean it?" Dr. Allstrom might not typically play favorites, but the research team was less a team working together and more a pit of competitors jostling each other for primacy. "That's awfully solid of you."

Mikki shrugged. "Karma. I'd want someone to do it for me. So, come on," she waved him toward the metal table and smiled.

They bent their heads over the binder and silently reviewed the procedure for isolating the cortical gray matter that they would need for comparison to the demyelinated gray matter already fixed on the slides from the recently deceased patients with dementia.

After Troy was confident he had a handle on their task, he looked sidelong at Mikki. "It's amazing, isn't it?"

"This is the missing piece. This is *it,* Troy." Her voice shook with enthusiasm.

"I'm so glad Dr. Allstrom was able to convince the family and treating physician. I was concerned they wouldn't consent given their religious beliefs." Troy gave voice to the worry that had niggled at him all night long.

"What do you mean? Mrs. Chevitz was already enrolled." She wrinkled her forehead and gaze him a questioning look.

"Right, but she's an observant Jew. The Jewish religion has a prohibition against autopsy. Dr. Allstrom said she was going to talk to the clinician and explain how important Mrs. Chevitz's sample is to our work."

Her curious expression morphed into one of concern. "Are you sure? About the autopsy prohibition, I mean."

"Yeah. I dated a girl whose family was super religious. Her dad was a rabbi." He laughed at the memory. "Boy, did he hate my Episcopal butt."

"If that's the case, then why are the Chevitzes allowing the autopsy?" Mikki pressed.

He answered slowly. "I'm not an expert, but I know there are exceptions to the ban on desecrating the body. I guess Dr. Kayser explained how many productive lives could potentially be extended if the medicine makes it to the market. It's a close question, because I always thought *halakhah* would usually only make an exception if the autopsy could save a specific, known person. Or … something like that. Also, I guess it would depend on if she's Orthodox, Reform, or Conservative. They have different beliefs—it's almost like the differences between the various Protestant denominations."

"What's *halakhah*?"

"Jewish law. But, anyway, it's awesome that they signed the consent."

She gnawed at her lower lip for a second and then wheeled her stool around to grab a folder off the desk behind her. She flipped through it twice before she looked up at him with a pained expression. "There's no consent in here, Troy."

They stared at each other in mutual dismay for a moment.

"I'm sure she got one," he finally said.

"What if she didn't?"

He shook his head, rejecting the very idea. "She must have. I'm sure she would have. She was going to talk to Dr. Kayser when I left to come over here last night."

"I guess she did," she agreed halfheartedly.

Troy's thrill of anticipation turned into a blanket of anxiety. He ignored the cold clench in the pit of his stomach and turned back to the binder, pretending he was reading the protocol again and pretending not to feel Mikki's worried eyes boring into the back of his head. After a few moments of silence, she slipped off her stool and left the room. He kept his eyes on the page in front of him.

~ ~ ~ ~ ~ ~ ~ ~ ~ ~

Al Kayser woke from his four-hour nap and checked the time on the bedside clock. Six o'clock on the dot. He picked up the phone and pressed the zero button.

"Good morning, Golden Village," the calm voice of the weekend receptionist said, smooth as silk.

"Good Morning, Ella. This is Dr. Kayser. How's my patient doing?"

"Mrs. Chevitz? The attendant just checked on her. She's sleeping peacefully. Her kids ... not so much," her voice dropped a notch and took on a mournful note.

"I'd imagine. These next days will be hard for them, there's no doubt about that. I'll get cleaned up and head over. Will you let them know I'm on my way?"

"Will do. Do you have everything you need? I can send an aide over with towels or toiletries."

"I always keep an overnight kit in the car," he assured her, "so I'm all set. But I appreciate the offer. I'm just thankful you folks are kind enough to let me use a vacant cottage in situations like this."

"Oh, Dr. Kayser, *we're* so grateful to *you* for taking such good care of our guests."

He hung up and headed to the bathroom, his spirits buoyed by the genuine appreciation in Ella's voice. He washed his face, shaved, and brushed his teeth with the series of economical movements he'd used every day since his long-ago residency. He locked up the room and returned his Dopp kit to his trunk, then crossed the lawn to the main building. Once inside, he greeted Ella and checked his watch. *6:10 a.m.*

As he started toward the hallway to Adina's room, the main lobby doors opened with a pneumatic whine, and the sound of running feet hitting the tile floor echoed through the space. Ella's welcoming smile turned frosty at the disturbance, and Al glanced over his shoulder to see his a young Japanese woman sprinting toward him. Her white lab coat billowed out, and her long, loose dark hair trailed behind her like kite tails.

"Dr. Kayser? Are you Dr. Kayser?" she called.

Ella sprang out of her chair. "Young lady, please lower your voice," she scolded with as much disapproval as Al had ever heard her muster.

"I'm sorry," the woman stage whispered as a crimson stain worked its way up her neck to her cheeks. She closed the gap between herself and him, "Are you Dr. Kayser?" she repeated softly.

"I am."

A ripple of relief rolled across her face. "Oh, thank goodness. Mikki Yotamora," she said, sticking out her hand.

"Ms. Yotamora," he said then corrected himself after glancing at her embroidered coat pocket, "I beg your pardon, Dr. Yotamora. What can I do for you?"

She caught her breath and seemed to screw up her courage before answering. "I'm doing graduate work for Dr. Greta Allstrom. I'm on her research team."

Al didn't know what she'd say next, but instinct told him it wouldn't be good. "I see," he said to prompt her.

"Dr. Allstrom had me come into the lab very early this morning to prep for some important brain tissue slices she expects to receive today."

His stomach dropped. "Not from Adina Chevitz?"

She nodded. Her eyes were wide and sad. "Another researcher and I were chatting while we worked, and he mentioned that it was lucky that the Chevitz family had agreed to the donation because their religion prohibits autopsy. Is he correct?"

"I think you know he is. That's why you're here, isn't it? To warn me?" he asked gently.

"I ... I'm here because I'm concerned. I wanted to double check. The only consent form in our file is several years old. It permits blood draws. I thought, maybe, there was an oversight and the consent to harvest brain tissue was left in her room or something." She said the words haltingly, as if she were searching for some reasonable explanation for her boss's behavior.

"I assure you they were not. Adina Chevitz is a very religious woman, and her Jewish faith is important to her. She did not consent to a post-mortem autopsy of her brain, as your lead researcher well knows."

Mikki Yotamora's lower lip quivered. "She's critical to our study. It's so important that we compare our results to her gray matter to see—"

His anger flared. "Did Dr. Allstrom send you over here to wheedle me?"

"What? No. No, she doesn't know I'm here. Please, you can't tell her." The color drained from the woman's face.

"I promise not to mention it," he assured her as his rage at Dr. Allstrom subsided in the face of her student's obvious fear. "Would you like to speak to Mrs. Chevitz's son and confirm for yourself that she doesn't wish to participate?"

"No, I can't do that." She had the expression of a trapped animal, unable to flee but aware that she was stuck.

"Okay, let's do this. You wait here, and I'll double check. I give you my word that if the family is willing to allow the brain study, I'll get you a signed informed consent form."

She nodded. "Thank you. Please explain that she's the missing piece. If we can see her gray matter and compare it to the gray matter of the patients who took the supplement, we'll be leaps and bounds closer to getting our drug to market. It's *so* crucial."

"I'll tell the family."

He left the graduate student standing in the hall and gave soft tap on Adina's door.

"Come in," she called in a shaky voice.

Her sons and daughters were arranged in a semi-circle around her bed, with red-rimmed, puffy eyes. He nodded to the children and then crossed the room to clasp Adina's hand.

"How are you this morning, dear?"

"I'm ready, Dr. Kayser. Whenever He is, I am." She smiled, then her gaze shifted to her family. "They'll take good care of each other, I know."

"We will, Mother," Ruth sobbed.

Al puffed out his cheeks and exhaled. "I have to ask you a question, Adina."

She nodded, looking up at him with clear brown eyes, still smiling.

"The researchers who come in and take blood samples every now and again, you know who I mean?"

"Yes, sure."

"They're very interested in your brain."

"It's a good brain," she agreed solemnly.

"It is a good brain. It's served you well. And they're trying to understand how to help folks whose brains aren't as long-lasting and healthy as yours is in the later years. They think your brain might hold the key."

"Alzheimer's. Dementia. I've lost lots of friends to the fog of their memories. More than I can count."

He was sure she had. "I told the researchers that your Jewish faith prohibits any post-mortem study of your brain because I believe that to be true. But I'm certainly not a rabbinical scholar, and they're very eager. So I told them I would confirm with you. Are you willing to let them have a part of your brain?" He continued to hold her soft, warm wrinkled hands in his as he spoke, and she neither stiffened nor reacted visibly to the question.

Her son made a guttural, wordless shout of surprise, and Ruth's sisters joined her in a long wail. But Adina shushed them all. "I can't think over that noise. Quiet yourselves." She tilted her head and blinked at him from behind her oversized, once-fashionable glasses. "It's not *just* my brain, is it? I mean, they could look at a gentile's brain to answer this, yes?"

"Yes," he agreed. "As I understand their work, they need brain tissue from a mentally competent member of the study who didn't take their supplement. That's the control group. There surely aren't many of you, but you aren't the only control."

She thought for a long moment. "Then, no, I'm afraid I can't help them. It would be a *mitzvah*, perhaps. But, no, it's not natural. I've lived a good, faithful life. I want a good, faithful death. Don't leave my body alone. Call the burial society right away. Get me in the ground as soon as you can. Sit the *shiva*." She had turned toward her children and was speaking directly to Ralph.

"I will, Mother," he promised.

"I hope I haven't upset you," Al said.

"No, I'm not upset." Adina released his hand, shrugged her narrow shoulders, and raised her palms to the ceiling. "You don't ask, you don't get."

He laughed and patted her arm, "I'll let them know. I'll be back in a bit."

As the door closed behind them, she called, "Tell them I said *mazel tov!*"

Mikki Yotamora pitched forward expectantly when she saw him. "Did she agree?"

"No. She's adamant about her wishes. No autopsy. She wishes you good luck with your work, but she can't help you."

The young woman lowered her head and seemed to collapse in on herself, scooping her spine and shoulders into a C. "Thank you for asking." Then she looked up with a spark of fear. "What do I do about the standing order? I can't cancel it. Only Dr. Allstrom has authority."

"What order?"

"With the on-call morgue. She already put in the papers. That's why Troy's sitting in the lab waiting. Everything's in place."

"You go back to the lab. Don't tell anyone you talked to me. I'll take care of the rest," he muttered darkly.

She nodded.

As she turned to go, he stopped her. "You were right to come find me. That inner voice that told you to do it—don't let it fade. You'll need it again in your career, trust me. As long as you keep listening to it, it'll be there."

23.

ASHA AND CONNELLY WERE SNUGGLED under a thick, fleece blanket, each holding a sleepy baby, and waiting for the sun to begin its rise over Cadillac Mountain when Naya called.

"You're kidding," he said when Naya's distinctive ringtone—the Batman theme—sounded from deep within Sasha's pocket.

She fumbled in her pocket for the phone and answered in a loud whisper. "What's wrong?"

"Why do you always have to assume something's wrong?"

"Because I'm freezing my butt off on the top of a mountain waiting for the earliest sunrise on the East Coast. Which means *you're* freezing your butt off in the pre-dawn light, because the sun won't rise there for at least another forty-five minutes, maybe longer. So, either you haven't gone to bed yet or you're already up. Neither one is likely to be good news. Unless you and Carl ran off and eloped. Are you calling me from Vegas?"

Naya snorted. "No surprise nuptials. But, yeah, I guess something's wrong. Sorry to interrupt your family getaway."

Oh, don't be. It's already been pretty well ruined by the knowledge that my shady father-in-law wants my husband, the father of my children, to undergo major surgery to save his life, Sasha thought. What she said was, "Don't worry about it. I know you wouldn't call if it weren't important. What's going on?"

Connelly was gawking at her as if she were out of her mind, making big, looping arm gestures toward the horizon, as if she were going to somehow miss the spectacle. She gave him a withering look before turning to pin her eyes on the orb revealing itself in the sky while keeping the phone pressed firmly against her ear.

"Actually, I've got Dr. Kayser on hold. I'm going to patch him in and he can explain it, okay?"

"Sure thing."

While Naya added Dr. Kayser to the call, Sasha turned to her husband. "Look, something's wrong. I have to take this. I promise I'll watch the sun come up while I talk to them."

He just shook his head. "You'll be missing out. Whatever it is can wait a few minutes, can't it?"

She pinched the phone between her shoulder and neck and raised her palms skyward. "I don't know. Maybe not."

Just then, Dr. Kayser's apologetic voice sounded in her ear. "Sasha, I'm so sorry to bother you. I didn't know you were on vacation."

"First of all, I'm your lawyer. You're supposed to call me if you need me. Second of all, it's not really a vacation. It's more of ... a personal errand. Anyhow, you and Naya are up very early. Who wants to tell me what the issue is?"

"Actually, Dr. Kayser hasn't gone to bed yet," Naya interjected.

"Really? Why?" Sasha asked.

"I napped. I have a patient who is about to leave this mortal coil. It's a matter of hours, maybe a day at most, at this point. I've been at her bedside with her family since last night," he explained.

"Let me guess. She's on the locked dementia unit at Golden Village," Sasha posited.

"Close, but no cigar. Adina Chevitz *is* a resident of Golden Village but she hasn't exhibited any signs of dementia. She recently moved from an independent living cottage to the main wing because her physical health was failing," he said.

"Okay." Sasha waited for either her associate or her client to explain the reason for the call.

Naya prompted the doctor. "Dr. Kayser had a run-in with Dr. Allstrom last night."

He made a small sound of protest. "I wouldn't call it a run-in. She caught up with me in the hall outside Mrs. Chevitz's room and asked me if she could talk to the family because Adina is enrolled in her study."

"You think she was asking if she could talk to them about taking a sample of her brain?"

"Almost certainly, which given her past practices, is great progress. But her timing was just terrible. The family was gathered around the bed so Mrs. Chevitz could say the last prayer."

"Last rites?"

"No, last prayer. They're Jewish. After the prayer, the dying person shouldn't be left alone. The family, of course, stayed, but they asked me to be there, too. So I also spent the night. Around two in the morning, she was resting comfortably, so I availed myself of one of the vacant cottages and had a short rest. When I returned to the main building, a young woman, a Dr. Yotamora, chased me down. She was quite agitated."

"Who is she?" Sasha asked, unable to place the name. She raised her free hand and shielded her eyes from the brilliant light that spread across the sky. Beside her, Connelly inhaled, a sharp intake of breath.

"She's a graduate student working on Greta Allstrom's team."

"Interesting," Sasha remarked.

"Oh, it gets better," Naya promised.

"She explained to me that she and one of her colleagues had gotten in to the lab very early this morning to wait for the delivery of some important brain tissue slices. While they waited, they chatted. In the course of conversation, her coworker mentioned that it was lucky that the Chevitz family had agreed to the donation despite their religion's prohibition on autopsy. Ms. Yotamora became concerned because the only consent form in the file was the earlier form agreeing to participate in the blood draws."

"I can't believe even Allstrom would try to pull something like this. I mean, this is really brazen," Sasha said.

"Brazen is a good word for it. Desperate is another. From what I gathered, Mrs. Chevitz's brain is particularly important to the study because Adina doesn't have dementia. But Dr. Allstrom can't just *take* it. I explained to Ms. Yotamora that, as far as I knew, neither Mrs. Chevitz not her family had been asked, let alone given consent. I offered to let her speak to Mrs. Chevitz's oldest son, who's making many of the decisions, but she demurred."

"Why?" Sasha wondered aloud.

"She's scared. She's rightfully worried that Dr. Allstrom is going to be furious with her for coming to me. And she knows I'm powerless to protect her from university politics if the study falls apart because she acted. Meeting with a member of the Chevitz family would have just entangled her further in the whole morass. I understand her predicament. I did pop my head into the room and ask Adina herself, who was awake at that point. She emphatically does not want to be autopsied and certainly doesn't want her brain to be harvested. I set off a round of wailing among her children. They're an observant family, and the idea is abhorrent to them. I explained this to Mikki Yotamora, thanked her for her courage in seeking me out, and sent her back to her lab. I told her I'd handle it from here. But, aside from barricading Adina's door, I'm not sure what to do. I tried to reach Athena, but she didn't answer her phone. Of course, it is very early in the morning. But I don't think Athena is the best person to resolve this, anyway," Dr. Kayser finished in a mournful tone.

He might not be sure what to do next, but Sasha was. And, as Naya proved with her very next sentence, she was, too.

"I already called and checked. The emergency judge this weekend is Nolan. I can get started on a TRO as soon as we hang up. I'll have a draft to you in a couple hours."

"Don't reinvent the wheel," Sasha told her. "Crib from papers on the system and go light on the details. The salient facts should be plenty to get the order—the family's religious beliefs prohibit an autopsy. We have reason to believe that Allstrom intends to violate those beliefs."

"I'm a little confused. I thought we couldn't file a complaint," Dr. Kayser said.

"This changes everything. The Chevitz family is a real plaintiff, facing a very real harm. Assuming they'll agree to cooperate in the litigation, of course."

"Oh, they will. They were pleading with me to do whatever I could to stop this."

"Okay. Naya will put together an emergency motion asking the court to enter a TRO—a temporary restraining order—preventing Dr. Allstrom from harvesting Adina Chevitz's brain tissue. She'll send it to me to review and I'll sign off on it. We'll probably need affidavits from you and Mrs. Chevitz to support the motion—"

"What about Mikki Yotamora?" Naya broke in.

"Eventually, it'll be unavoidable. But I think we can get the temporary order without involving her.

Let's not spook her now. Dr. Kayser, once we have final papers, Naya will bring them to Golden Village and go over them with you and the family. Then we'll get them on file. We could have an order in hand by lunchtime, certainly before dinner."

"I can't thank you enough," he said. "The Chevitz family will be so relieved."

"No worries," Sasha said. "Just hang tight until Naya gets there."

They said their goodbyes, and Sasha and Naya waited for him to drop off the call.

"I'll get you a draft as fast I can," Naya said.

"I know." Sasha let her eyes drift over to Connelly's face. He was watching her and seemed to know what she was thinking. He nodded. "We're going to go back to the house, pack up, and change our flight. I'll be back in Pittsburgh by tonight, but in the unlikely event the court wants to have a hearing before I'm on the ground, you'll have to do it."

"No, don't cut your vacation short, Mac. I'll handle this. Trust me, I'm not conflicted any more. This Allstrom woman has gone too far. The hearing will probably be Monday, don't you think?"

"Probably. But, I'm coming back anyway. Connelly has something that came up, too. We were going to cut it short by a day. What's one more? Just get cracking."

Naya exhaled and laughed shakily. "Okay. Then, I'm not going to lie, I'll be glad to have you back in town. This is heavy. Some lady's dying wish?—I don't want to screw it up."

Me neither, Sasha thought.

"We won't," she said firmly.

24.

L EO WAS BIZARRELY GRATEFUL FOR
Sasha's work emergency. For one thing, it
meant they could return home even earlier
than they'd agreed, which would mean he could
start poking around in his father's background
sooner than he'd thought. For another, the flurry
of telephone calls and emails that she and Naya
were exchanging meant that she'd be occupied during the trip back to Pittsburgh and wouldn't want
to discuss Wynn/Nguyen and his request. Not yet,
at least. He trusted Sasha's judgment and valued
her input tremendously—as much as Hank's,
maybe even more. But he needed more time to process what had happened at the Blue House.

He glanced over at the driver's seat. She was
white-knuckling the steering wheel. The road was

clear and traffic was light, so he assumed her death grip was the result of stress over her case and not the driving conditions. But just in case, he asked, "Do you want to switch?"

"What? No. I should drive now, while Naya's revising the motion to include my edits. Once she emails me the revision, you can take over so I can read it."

He still didn't understand how she could read long, dense legal documents on the tiny smartphone screen, but more power to her.

"You seem a little tense," he observed.

She took her eyes off the interstate and gave him a look. "You think? Some rogue doctor's planning to cut up the brain of an old Jewish lady, and my husband's father wants his liver. I don't know why I'd be stressed." She lapsed into silence and then felt mildly guilty about the sarcasm. "Are they sleeping back there?" she asked, changing the subject.

He twisted in his seat to check. "Nope. Finn's staring at Fiona. And well, so is Fiona. She's transfixed, looking at her reflection in that toy attached to the carseat."

"Perfect. If they stay awake for this leg, I bet they'll both sleep on the plane."

"Amen to that."

They fell back into silence, and his thoughts returned to his father. He accepted that the man didn't want to establish a relationship with him. That fact infuriated Sasha, but it was inescapable. He couldn't force Wynn to be paternal, and, at this point, he wasn't sure what he needed a father for anyway. He had Hank, who was a mentor and guide. Sasha's dad doted on the twins and provided any support he and Sasha might ask for, which wasn't much—maybe an extra set of hands during a home improvement project. So Wynn's emotional distance didn't really bother him. Sure, it was odd to know he was connected through DNA and bloodlines to a stranger, but that weirdness aside, nothing had changed in his actual day-to-day existence as a result of knowing that Wynn was the man who impregnated his mother.

Except, of course, for the favor. The favor complicated things. If Wynn could be trusted, he was dying. Leo was inclined to believe him because he *seemed* sick and weak. When Leo looked closely at the man, he could see the faint ghost of a once hale and powerful Doug Wynn, but the man he met was anything but. And, again, if he took him at his word, Leo could save his life. In fact, he *expected* Leo to save his life, no questions asked.

Leo conceded that Wynn had a point. Even though he didn't teach Leo how to fish or take him to his first baseball game, the reality was that, if not for Doug Wynn, Leo wouldn't be alive. But now he, too, was a father. And a husband. He had to weigh those roles.

The issue was also clouded by Leo's suspicion that Doug Wynn may not be the most upstanding of citizens. In addition to the gruesome *punji* trap in Wynn's yard and the possibility that Wynn had killed or otherwise caused his messenger to disappear, there was the fact that even Hank, with all his connections and access, had been able to uncover no real, traceable background on the man. Perhaps running Duc Nguyen through the databases would prove more fruitful. But even more than these red flags, Leo had a feeling about him. Wynn reminded him, in some ephemeral, unprovable way, of all the terrorists, thieves, and murderers he encountered in his work. It was just a hunch, but he didn't intend to ignore it.

Regardless of what, if anything, he learned about his father's past, he was going to have to make a decision. He turned and studied Sasha's profile. Could he risk undergoing major surgery if it meant he might die and miss out on a lifetime with his spitfire of a wife? If it meant he might not see Finn and Fiona take their first steps, ride a bike, graduate from college? His eyes grew damp and he blinked quickly, willing himself to pull it together.

"What are you thinking?" Sasha asked, giving him a curious sidelong glance.

"That I love you."

"And I love you," she answered as her cell phone blared to life. Batman again. "That's Naya. I have to take it. Why don't I pull over and you can drive for awhile?"

"Sure thing," he agreed in a forced, cheerful voice, as he banished all thoughts of Doug Wynn and his cancerous liver from his mind.

25.

GRETA DIDN'T WANT TO BE crass, but she couldn't help wishing Mrs. Chevitz would hurry up and die already. The woman was just lingering at this point.

She checked her watch. It was nearly four in the afternoon, almost a full day after Adina Chevitz's family arrived to say their goodbyes. She put her container of soup in the microwave and pressed the button to heat it. Just as she was thinking that she ought to call over to the lab and send poor Mikki home until further notice, the door to the physician's lounge swung open.

She glanced up, expecting to see Athena or one of the staff coming in to take a late lunch or early dinner break. Instead, Naya Andrews, the African-

American attorney, stood in the doorway smiling right at her. Greta instinctively stiffened.

"Can I help you?"

"You absolutely can," Naya answered in a gleeful tone. She took three quick strides and quickly crossed the room. "This is for you." She pressed a manila envelope into Greta's hand. "I can't believe I finally get to say this in real life. You've been served."

Greta stared blankly at her for several beats before she turned her gaze down to the envelope she was now holding. "I ... don't understand."

"Right. I bet you don't. That's okay; let me make it crystal clear so there's no confusion. Today, Adina Chevitz filed a motion for an emergency temporary restraining order against you."

"Against me?" Greta's legs started to buckle and she leaned against the refrigerator for support. "There must be some sort of mistake."

"There's no mistake. United States District Judge Pamela Nolan granted the order less than an hour ago. Her order, as issued, enjoins you from interfering in any way with the prompt burial of her body in compliance with Jewish law; specifically, you are forbidden to cause any part of her body, including, but not limited to, her brain tissue to be autopsied, biopsied, or sampled or to in any way desecrate her corpse. Any attempt on your part to do so—or to otherwise go against Mrs. Chevitz's religious beliefs and stated wishes—will be a violation of a federal court order." The woman rattled off the legalese from memory and with evident relish.

"She enrolled in the study," Greta said weakly, as the prospect of moving forward—which had been so close, so real—evaporated.

"That's right. She enrolled in a study that entailed giving periodic blood samples while alive. That doesn't conflict with her religious beliefs. A post-mortem brain tissue slice would. I'm going to leave a copy of the order at the front desk and advise the staff as to its contents. If Mrs. Chevitz should happen to die this weekend, they will be instructed to turn her body over as quickly as practical to the Jewish burial society with which her family contracted. We're serving the university, too, but the legal department is unlikely to look at the order before Monday. If I were you, I'd get in touch with your boss right now and explain the situation because the judge is likely to hold a hearing first thing Monday. That's a little piece of free advice from me to you."

Greta stared mutely at the woman. Her entire body had gone numb.

The attorney turned on her heel and walked out of the room.

After several moments, Greta fumbled in her pocket and took out her phone. The Andrews woman was right, she should call her boss. But her finger hesitated over the contact card for Virgil Buxton. Instead, she pressed it down on a different contact entry.

"The Alpha Fund," an unaccented female voice answered in a bored tone.

"This is Dr. Greta Allstrom. I have ... a problem."

26.

SASHA WAS BREWING COFFEE WHEN she heard a soft tapping at the front door.

"I'll get it," Connelly called from the front of the house.

A moment later, she heard Naya's greeting and then the low murmur of voices as Connelly no doubt confirmed Naya's hunch that the twins were sleeping soundly upstairs. The pair came into the kitchen as she was stretched up on her tiptoes trying to reach the largest of the oversized coffee mugs.

She turned and shot her husband a look. "You must have unloaded the dishwasher last. I can't reach them." She harbored a growing suspicion that he intentionally put items out of her reach for his own amusement.

"Let me get those for you, short stuff. You want some coffee, Naya?"

"I believe I do."

Sasha raised a brow at that. Naya rarely drank caffeine this late in the day. "Are you about to crash?"

"I think so. My adrenaline was really pumping, but as soon as I served Dr. Allstrom, I got so sleepy."

"Makes sense. Have a seat and tell me all about it. Was she furious?"

Naya let herself fall into one of the kitchen chairs. "No, more like stunned."

Connelly took three mugs down and started pouring coffee into them while Sasha joined Naya at the table. "Did you tell Dr. Kayser he could go home?" she asked.

Naya shook her head. "He actually can't. It's still *Shabbat* until sundown. If Mrs. Chevitz dies, he's going to have to make the arrangements for the family. They can't do any work on their Sabbath."

"Surely there's an exception for handling a death."

"You'd think so, wouldn't you? The fact that this all went down on *Shabbat* really complicated things." She reached up and took the coffee mug from Connelly's hands.

Sasha shared her eagerness. "Thanks, babe," she said, taking her own steaming mug from her husband. "What things?" she asked Naya.

"All the things. Like, for instance, at first Mrs. Chevitz's son said she couldn't possibly sign her affidavit because writing is work."

"How'd you get around that one?"

Naya took a sip of the hot coffee before responding. "It took a while. Dr. Kayser and I tried to convince the children that Jewish law would have to make an exception in this instance, but they wouldn't budge. I was beginning to think I was going to have to file it unsigned with an explanatory footnote and hope she lived past the Sabbath so she could sign it and I could update the filing."

Sasha grimaced. "Ugh."

"I know, right? But, Adina Chevitz woke up in the middle of all the handwringing and asked what was going on." Naya chuckled. "She's sharp as a tack, by the way. She said 'give me the blasted papers.' She read the affidavit, twice, carefully and then signed it with her left hand."

Connelly, who'd been rummaging in the refrigerator, came over to the table bearing a plate of cheese, olives, and nuts. "Here. Nibble. You two are going to need protein if you're working through the night, which I suspect you are. But what's the significance of signing left handed?"

"Apparently, there are all these exceptions for a woman who goes into labor on the Sabbath. Mrs. Chevitz's fourth child was born around midnight on a Friday and she signed her admission forms to the labor and delivery unit in 1956 with her non-dominant hand on the advice of her then-rabbi. She declared that an exception that applied to entering the world ought to apply to exiting it. And that was that."

"Thank goodness." Sasha picked up a handful of nuts and turned to smile at Connelly. "Thanks for the snacks."

"You're welcome. Are you two planning to go into the office or are you going to work here?"

"I think we have everything we need to do it from here, and it'll be more comfortable," she answered.

"Okay, in that case, I have to run an errand. I'll be back in a bit." He leaned down, kissed her forehead, and then walked out of the kitchen before she could ask any questions about his errand.

"What was that all about?" Naya asked, popping an olive into her mouth.

Probably Doug Wynn, Sasha thought.

"I'm not sure," she said.

27.

HANK LOOKED AS TIRED AS Leo felt. So tired, that he regretted showing up unannounced at his boss's home on a Saturday night.

"If this isn't a good time—" he began, but Hank waved the rest of the sentence away.

"I could use some adult conversation. Want a beer?"

"Definitely."

"Come on, then. I'll get us some cold ones and we can sit out back on the deck. That way you can fill me in on your trip up north without us having to worry about waking the kids." Hank led him through the first floor to the kitchen in the back of the house.

"The big ones can't be sleeping already," Leo remarked. The six children who Hank had adopted ranged in age from five to eighteen

"No, they're not. Cole is out with his friends, and the middle two are streaming a movie. But the little ones are sleeping. Let's keep it that way." He reached into the refrigerator and pulled out two bottles. He twisted the cap off one, passed it to Leo, opened his own, and then headed for the back deck.

Leo followed, making sure the screen door didn't bang shut behind him.

"So," Hank asked as he took a seat at the patio table, "was the visit to Wynn fruitful? Does he actually know anything about your father?"

"You could say that." Leo pulled out the chair across from Hank and lowered himself into it. "Whatever else he is, though, Doug Wynn's not former law enforcement." He leaned back and let the bracing night air flow over the day's growth on his chin. The effect was the same as taking a power nap. Instant energy.

"You sure about that? Nobody but a spook would have a completely blank slate."

"I'm positive. And that's not entirely true," Leo countered.

"For example?"

"Your slumbering angels, for one, would turn up as blanks in a search."

"You think he's in witness protection?" Hank cocked his head. He'd adopted the Bennett children after their mother had been murdered despite being enrolled in the federal witness protection program.

"Maybe. He's definitely opposed to folks dropping by uninvited."

"What makes you say that?"

Leo took a long pull on his bottle before answering. He savored the icy liquid's journey down his throat. Then he said, "For starters, the *punji* pit in his backyard."

Hank's bottle hit the glass-topped table with a thud. "A *punji* pit. You're serious, aren't you?"

"As cancer." He laughed darkly. "Which, by the way, he has."

"Who? Wynn or your dad?"

"Wynn is my dad." Leo couldn't tell if Hank was speechless or just searching for words that weren't profane. He'd been on a no-swearing kick because the two youngest Bennetts had been parroting some colorful phrases. Either way, after listening to the crickets singing in the bushes for nearly a full minute, he decided to plow ahead with the rest of the story. "His real name is Duc Nguyen, and he's dying of liver cancer."

"Man. Talk about a gut punch," Hank managed. His face sagged, as if it had absorbed the sadness of the news.

"Oh, there's more. I can save him."

"What? How?"

"He wants me to become a living liver donor. The doctors will remove a portion of my liver and transplant it to him."

By the dim glow of the light filtering through the kitchen window, he saw Hank's eyes widen. "Then what?"

"Then, both halves regenerate. Apparently, I'm back to normal in no time, and he recovers, too."

"Are you considering doing it?"

There it was. The money question. "Am I considering it? Yeah, I'm thinking about it. But I need to research the transplant procedure, talk to some experts. And I'd like to see if I can't learn a bit more about Duc Nguyen first, now that we have a real name."

"You think he's hiding something? Plenty of folks Americanize their names." Hank narrowed his eyes and studied Leo's face.

"Sure, lots of people do that. Not a lot of people have ambushes set up around their homes. Not a lot of people come up as blanks in *your* search results. Not a lot of people pay cash for their houses. I'd wager very few people do all of them."

"I get it, smart ass," Hank conceded. "You think he's hiding from someone?"

"Yeah. He's living in an extremely remote location, on a hard-to-access island. The house has a million-dollar view of Somes Sound and the mountains in Acadia National Park but it's completely screened by trees. Then there's the cloak-and-dagger way he contacted me. There's something going on there."

"Maybe he's former Viet Cong?"

Leo shook his head. "No. My mom was clear about that much: he was a South Vietnamese civilian. But he puts off ... a vibe. My gut says he got mixed up in something when he came here."

"Any idea when that was?"

"According to him, he was already in the United States when I took my trip over there looking for him. That was in '85. So, before then." Leo raised his bottle to his lips and was surprised to find that it was empty. He returned it to the table.

"You want another?"

"No, thanks. There's something else."

"Let's hear it."

"There was a Honda Civic in his shed. He lent it to me to drive back down to the town and told me to leave it in the ferry parking lot. I didn't think much of it, but Sasha saw a poster about a missing car. And apparently, unrelatedly, there's a missing kid from New York last seen on the island. The guy's description matched the messenger who showed up at my house last week."

Hank rubbed his temple as if the conversation was giving him a headache. "You think he literally killed the messenger?"

"All I know is there's a missing guy. And Wynn may have had me move a car that could be tied to a crime off his property. I hate to ask you to go back to the well, but can you run him again? I'm going to work some other angles, but you have better access than I do to the official channels."

"Of course I'll put him through the databases and see what pops. But you be careful freelancing. If he is a bad dude, you don't know what kind of viper's nest you might disturb if you go poking around." Hank's forehead creased with worry.

"I know." Leo stood. "I should get going. Thank you."

Hank got to his feet. "Any time. You know, it sounds like one heck of a crap storm just blew into your life. But, hey, you found your father. That's something good."

Leo opened his mouth to explain that the man who'd sired him had no intention of playing a father role, even if he did decide to donate part of his liver. But it was late, he was tired, and, to be honest, he didn't feel like unpacking his feelings. So he clamped his mouth shut and nodded.

28.

ASHA NEVER IMAGINED THAT THERE would come a day when she'd view a trip to Target to pick up laundry detergent and cat food as a romantic getaway. But that day had come, and it was today. She linked her arm through Connelly's and snuggled into his side.

"It feels weird to be walking through here with my hands free. Your parents are the best."

She smiled. It *had* been a nice surprise when her father had insisted they leave the babies with him and go 'do something,' while her mom put together Sunday dinner. She'd tried to demur and offered to help her mother in the kitchen, but Val had swatted her out of the room with a tea towel.

So here they were, strolling through the store, each with a cup of overpriced coffee in hand. They stopped in the Halloween aisle—Sasha to browse decorations, Connelly to browse family-sized bags of peanut butter cups. He dumped an armload of candy into the basket.

"How many trick-or-treaters do you think we're going to get?" She cast a dubious look at the pile of bags.

"Who cares? We can freeze the leftovers."

"We'd better start running again."

He laughed but didn't disagree.

She held up two tiny jack-o-lantern costumes. "What do you think?"

"Definitely. I think they have pet costumes, too. Hang on." He disappeared down the next aisle.

Pet costumes? Mocha, maybe. But if he thought he was coaxing Java into a Halloween costume, he'd better trade some of his chocolates for canned tuna.

She was heading after him to share her perspective when her cell phone vibrated in her bag. She stopped near a display of black-and-orange wreaths and dug it out of her bag. Dr. Kayser's contact information filled the display.

"Hi, Dr. Kayser."

"Good morning, Sasha. I'm calling to let you know Adina Chevitz has passed away early this morning." His voice was tired.

"I'm sorry."

"She was ready. And she hung in until after the Sabbath had ended, so her family was able to get in touch with their rabbi and the burial society. Her body's already been removed, and she'll be buried by the end of the day."

"That's fast. Is it because of Allstrom?"

"Not really. Their beliefs include burying the body as quickly as possible."

She half-listened to his explanation while she considered the ramifications of Mrs. Chevitz's death on the temporary restraining order.

"Sasha?" he asked when the silence extended a bit too long.

"I'm here. I'm just thinking this through."

"Do you mean how this development affects the case?"

"Precisely."

Connelly appeared with a small, satiny devil costume in one hand and a cape and bat ears in the other. She couldn't suppress a grin at his silliness but put up a finger to let him know not to interrupt her. He nodded his understanding, added the costumes to the basket she'd rested on the floor then picked it up and wandered off—no doubt taking advantage of her call to load up on more candy.

"Will the hearing go forward as planned tomorrow?" Dr. Kayser asked.

"That depends on us. The issue is effectively moot, so the TRO should be dissolved as a matter of course. All it would take is a phone call. But ..."

"Yes?"

"We *could* show up at the appointed time and ask Judge Nolan to modify and expand the order to prohibit Dr. Allstrom from harvesting brain tissue from *anyone* without first obtaining specific informed consent."

"Will the judge do that?"

"Possibly. Technically, she probably ought to dissolve the TRO, dismiss the case, and tell us to file a new motion for injunctive relief. But Judge Nolan is one of the more pragmatic judges on the Western District bench. There's a decent chance she'd grant the request temporarily and schedule a hearing on that order later in the week."

"Should we try?"

"I don't see a downside. We've already teed up the issue. The worst she can say is 'no.' But there's no reason for the Chevitz family to come to court tomorrow. I'm sure they have other priorities right now, anyway."

"They certainly do. But should we try to find another family? I could check in with my patients at Golden Village to see who else might have a religious or philosophical objection."

"Eventually, maybe. But our trying to replace Adina Chevitz with a new named plaintiff in the existing TRO would definitely tick off the judge—it's too transparent. Our best move at this stage is to argue the order *isn't* mooted by Mrs. Chevitz's death and should be enlarged, not dissolved." It was a novel argument, but it could work. Maybe.

"Okay. So do I need to come to your office before the hearing to prepare or should I meet you at the courthouse?"

"I'd like to walk you through your testimony. The hearing's at ten. Can you be at my office by eight o'clock?"

"Of course."

"Perfect. See you in the morning, Dr. Kayser." She ended the call and went off in search of Connelly in hopes of checking out and leaving the store before he decided that the adult, human members of their family needed to celebrate Halloween in costume as well.

29.

LEO HEARD SASHA'S LIGHT FOOTSTEPS falling along the hallway between the bedroom where the twins were sleeping and the small room he'd claimed as his home office. He quickly opened a new browser window and clicked on a random *Washington Post* headline as the door eased inward.

"Hey, are you coming to bed?" she asked in a low voice.

They seemed to spend a lot of time stage whispering, he realized. Occupational hazard as parents of twin infants.

"Just catching up on the news before I turn in." He swiveled to face her and gestured toward the monitor.

She glanced at the screen then perched on the edge of the desk and painted him with a knowing look. "Really? You're reading about the latest fall fashion trends?" She peered at the article. "I really don't think you could pull off fringe, honey."

He examined the screen more closely and tried to swallow a laugh. "Busted," he conceded.

"So what are you hiding?" She locked her big, green eyes on his and waited.

He moved the cursor over to the tab for the other window, clicked on it to reopen it, and watched her face as she read the title of the article. Amusement melted into worry.

"'What You Should Know if You're Considering Becoming a Living Donor?'" She moved her eyes from the screen and back to his face. "You're really considering it? Does that mean your father checked out?"

He pulled her off the desk and onto his lap before answering. "I'm still running him down, trying to find out more about his background. But, in the meantime, he needs an answer. So I'm learning what I can about the donation and transplant process. I'm working on parallel tracks."

Her mouth tightened and she stiffened, almost imperceptibly. "That makes sense." She exhaled shakily. "Okay, tell me about the process." She shifted in his lap to face him directly.

"Well the first thing I learned is that there's not a hospital in the state of Maine that performs living-donor liver transplants. There are fewer than a hundred places in the country that do it. But, luckily, one of them is right here in Pittsburgh."

"UPMC?"

"Right. So, if I were going to do this, I'd tell him that his doctor needs to refer him to UPMC's transplant program." It was a stroke of good fortune that one of the leading centers was local. It was almost a sign.

"Will he be accepted automatically?" she asked.

He shook his head. "No. He—and I—would both have to undergo a pre-transplant evaluation. There are specific criteria about how big his tumors can be, how numerous, whether the cancer has spread outside the liver ... that sort of thing. But I'd assume that if his treating physicians recommended the procedure, he probably qualifies."

"Probably," she agreed. "What about you?"

"I'd have to get a physical and have a psychiatric evaluation. Then I'd meet with a social worker to make sure I had support for when I left the hospital. They seem to require a fairly thorough vetting."

"I'm sure they do. It's a serious procedure ..."

She trailed off without asking the follow-up question, but he answered it anyway. "There aren't good numbers available on mortality rates for donors. But death is very rare."

"What about complications?"

He shrugged. "They happen. They're more likely to happen when the surgery occurs at a center that does a low-volume of living donor transplants. The surgeons at UPMC are more experienced than most, relatively speaking. And I'm young and healthy. I'm likely to come out of the surgery fine and be back to normal within a few months."

"It's still a big risk to take to save a stranger's life."

"He's not a stranger."

"He may as well be, Connelly."

He knew she was right as a factual matter. But he found himself viscerally reacting to the words. "He's not, though. He's my father."

She gnawed on her lower lip for a moment as if she was trying to decide whether to say what came next. "It sounds like you've already made up your mind. What if he really did kill that missing kid? You'd donate part of your liver to save a killer?"

"I still need to find out what kind of man my father is. Not because I think it changes anything, honestly, in the end. But it informs my decision. I just want to know who I'm doing this for," he answered. But as he spoke the words he realized she was right. He *had* already decided to agree to the transplant. The question felt settled, somehow.

She wrapped her arms around his neck and clung to him for several moments. He could feel the rapid flutter of her heartbeat against his chest. Then she loosened her grip and arched her neck and back to meet his eyes with her own, wet with unshed tears. "If this is what you have to do, I'll support you. You know that."

He pulled her close again and stroked her hair with one hand, unable to find the words to reassure her.

30.

Monday

SASHA WAS SHOWERING AND LEO was still contemplating getting out of bed when Hank called early Monday morning. Leo grabbed his cell phone before it rang a second time.

"Can you talk?" Hank asked.

"Yes."

"Sorry to call so early, but I put out some feelers over the weekend. The missing man on the flyer Sasha saw is a Chinese-American petty criminal by the name of Jake Wang. Last known address was an apartment in the Bronx."

"He has a sheet?" The kid hadn't struck him as particularly hardened or tough.

"Like I said, petty stuff. Receiving stolen property, a B&E at an auto parts store after hours. He was playing poker at an underground club when it was raided. According to arrest reports, he claimed to be affiliated with the Flying Dragons."

"Flying Dragons?"

"It's a Chinese gang that operates—well, used to operate in and around New York's Chinatown. Asian gangs had a stranglehold on the area in the 1980s and 90s. Flying Dragons, Ghost Boys, Born to Kill. It was before your time, but the feds made cleaning them up a priority. The remnants of the Flying Dragons are still lingering, but they're a shadow of what they once were. If this kid was mixed up with them, he was likely just a hanger-on. There's nothing in his sheet that screams gang-banger."

"Nothing that would make someone want to make him disappear," Leo agreed. Sasha emerged from the bathroom in her robe with a towel twisted around her wet hair. 'Hank' he mouthed.

She raised an imaginary mug to her mouth, asking if he wanted some coffee. He nodded 'yes,' and she cinched the robe's tie tighter around her waist and headed out of the room. Mocha and Java dove off the bed and followed her.

"Right. The kid's a wannabe. The missing person's report his parents filed said he told them he was traveling to Maine on business, but they didn't know any specifics about said business, except that he cadged his mom's credit card and used it to book a ferry passage to Great Cranberry Island," Hank continued.

"What about Duc Nguyen? Did anything pop when you ran his name? Any connection to Wang?"

"Apparently 'Duc Nguyen' is the 'John Smith' of Vietnamese names. I narrowed my search to men born between 1945 and 1955 named Duc Nguyen, still living, who immigrated to the United States between 1970 and 1985, and I got sixty-two hits."

"Sixty-two?"

"Yep. None of them live in Maine."

"Well, one of them does."

"First off, he's only included in that cohort if he's here legally. Second, he doesn't seem to have formally changed his name to Doug Wynn, because I can't tie the records I pulled on Doug Wynn to any of the sixty-two Nguyens."

"So, we've got nothing." Sixty-two Duc Nguyens would take weeks to run down. Weeks that one specific Duc Nguyen simply didn't have.

Sasha returned, walking slowly and deliberately, holding a full mug of steaming hot coffee in each hand. She passed one to him.

"Do you have anything else I can go on? Scars? Deformities? Unusual attributes?"

"He had the usual number of hands and feet. And he looks like an old Vietnamese guy, Hank."

"I have some other stuff on my plate this morning. If I get a chance, I'll comb through the Nguyen files and see if any of them are more interesting on a closer look, but don't hold your breath."

"Understood. Thanks."

"You can thank me when I get you some information."

Leo ended the call and placed the phone on the bedside table.

"Sounds like Hank didn't turn up anything new on your dad, huh? I'm sorry." Sasha rested her hand on his forearm.

He stared down at her hand, and an image of another hand that had recently rested in that same spot flashed through his mind—the wrinkled, frail hand of his father. Leo replayed the exchange with Wynn before he'd given Leo the car keys. The admonition not to take too long, and then the gesture with the upturned palms raised. Sitting on the edge of his bed, with his wife watching him with a concerned expression, Leo visualized something that hadn't registered in real time: A faded tattoo of three candles, a crudely drawn coffin, and the stylized letters 'B.T.K.'

"Connelly? Are you okay?"

He dragged himself back to the present and ignored his rapid pulse and rising heart rate. "I'm fine. I just had a thought. Hey, good luck today at the hearing."

She smiled uncertainly but kissed his cheek. "Thanks." She took her coffee and headed for the walk-in closet to get ready for her day. He took his coffee and tiptoed down the hallway to his office to run down his suspicion before the babies woke up.

~ ~ ~ ~ ~ ~ ~ ~ ~ ~ ~

"Here's where you've been hiding," Sasha said when she finally found Connelly hunched over his computer in the office. "I just fed the kids and changed their diapers. They're on the floor mat in the nursery working on their rolling skills. I have to run so I can get some work done before Dr. Kayser shows up." She leaned over the desk and kissed the top of his head. "Have a good day, okay?"

"You, too. Text me after court and let me know how it went."

"I will. Are you going to come over to the office this afternoon for their feeding?"

"I'll call first. Hey, do you still have the card that Annabeth woman gave you on the plane?"

Connelly's voice was casual—a little too casual. But she didn't have time to cross-examine him at the moment, so she simply dug Annabeth's card out of her wallet and handed it to him. "Here you go."

"Thanks."

She studied his face for a moment, but his expression was deliberately blank. "Connelly—" she began.

"I just have a question for her, Sasha. It's nothing major. Call it a hunch. I'll tell you all about it when I have details. Scout's honor," he said with an earnest smile.

"You do realize I know you were never a Boy Scout, right?"

He laughed and planted a kiss on her lips. "Go to work," he muttered with his mouth against hers.

"You're lucky I have somewhere I have to be. I have ways of making you talk," she replied.

"Is that a promise?" he countered in a husky voice.

"Definitely."

"Good."

"On that note, I'm leaving before I have to start all over again with my hair and makeup," she said

as she headed out of the office on surprisingly unsteady legs.

~ ~ ~ ~ ~ ~ ~ ~ ~ ~

As soon as Leo heard Sasha pull the front door
closed behind her, he picked up his phone and
called the number on Annabeth's card.

"Hello?" she answered.

"Annabeth Douglas?"

"Yes."

"This is Leo Connelly. My wife and I sat in the
same row as you last week on a flight to Portland."

"Yes, of course, I remember. Sasha and Leo, parents of newborn twins. How was your trip? Did you
make it to Acadia National Park?" She sounded
genuinely pleased to hear from him, if slightly surprised.

Leo forced himself to engage in the requisite
small talk while he laced his shoes and bundled the
twins into their one-piece hooded fleece blanket-
coat-things, packed up the diaper bag, and found
Mocha's leash.

When Annabeth paused to take a breath, he interrupted her story about her weekend visit with

her son. "I see on your card that you live in the North Hills."

"That's right," she answered cautiously.

"Have you ever been to Coffee Buddha on Perry Highway?"

"As a matter of fact, I have."

"Would you be willing to meet me there in about a half an hour? I'm buying."

She hesitated. "Leo ..."

He plowed forward. "Annabeth, please. I need to know everything you can tell me about the Vietnamese gang trial you mentioned that you covered in New York in 1994."

"Born to Kill?" Her tone changed from uncertain to intrigued.

"That's the one. In exchange for everything you can remember, I think I might be able to offer you a scoop."

"I'm retired, Leo." He heard her drumming her nails on a hard surface—a table or a desk. "But Coffee Buddha *does* pour a nice cup."

He smiled to himself. She might be retired but crime journalism was still in her blood.

"I'll meet you on their porch where they have the pet-friendly tables."

"Will Sasha be joining us?"

"I'm afraid not. She has a court appearance. I'll have Finn and Fiona, though. And our chocolate lab."

"Babies, a dog, the best coffee on this side of the river, *and* an audience to listen to me ramble about my glory days? You've got yourself a date with a reporter, Mr. Connelly."

31.

NAYA BARRELED INTO THE CONFERENCE room. "Still no sign of him," she said, snapping her fingers.

Sasha checked the time. 8:40. Dr. Kayser should have arrived forty minutes ago. If he walked through the door right this minute, they'd have *maybe* a half an hour to go over Mrs. Chevitz's affidavit and his testimony regarding the larger issue of consent before they had to head downtown to the courthouse.

She pressed her fingers against her temples and willed herself to stay calm. "Okay. Try his cell phone again."

Naya wrinkled her forehead and punched the number into the conference room phone. Within seconds, she was shaking her head. She dropped the phone back into its cradle. "Same as last time, Mac. It rolls straight to voicemail then I get the recording that his mailbox is full and not accepting messages."

They stared at each other in dismay for a full ten seconds. Then Sasha raised her shoulders and shrugged. "If we have to go without him, we'll figure something out. I'll call his office again."

She redialed the main number for Dr. Kayser's office and listened to the line ring. And ring. And ring. She was about to hang up, when a harried, breathless voice answered.

"Good morning. Doctor Kayser's office. Please—"

"Lucy, wait. Don't put me on hold."

"Attorney McCandless?" Lucy asked.

"Yes. Please tell me he's there?"

"He still hasn't shown up. He emailed last night and said to call and push back his morning appointments because he was going to be in court. If he did come in and do some paperwork early like he'd planned, he was already gone when I got here at seven thirty. Maybe he decided to meet you at the courthouse?" Her voice was a mixture of hope and worry. Sasha knew the feeling.

"Maybe," she allowed. "We'll head to the courthouse now, in case there was a mix-up and he's there. If you hear from him, please tell him to look for us there."

"I will," the receptionist promised. "And good luck."

"Thanks." She ended the call and turned to Naya, who was staring at her with wide, concerned eyes. "Let's pack it up and go. Maybe he got confused and went straight to court."

Naya twisted her mouth into a little moue of disbelief but said nothing.

"Or he was in a car accident. Or he met the woman of his dreams last night and is halfway to Tahiti. I don't know. He could be anywhere. What I do know is if *we* don't show up, Judge Nolan'll file a bar complaint so fast your head will spin. So get your stuff and let's go." Sasha wasn't kidding. Nolan had reported more attorneys to the bar for violations than the rest of the local bench combined.

Naya started packing up the files on autopilot. Sasha's pulse was racing and she could hardly breathe from worry but she hid her panic. She was the senior partner. Naya would take her cues from her. As long as Sasha acted as though it was no big deal that their sole witness was a no-show, they could just keep putting one foot in front of the other and muddle through.

For the first time in a long time, Sasha thought about her old mentor, Noah Peterson. Peterson had told her long ago that trial advocacy was one half bravado, one half theater, and one half law. She'd pointed out that that equation equaled three halves and he'd said, 'that's the kind of nitpicking that'll get you nowhere, Mac. If you're going to tell a judge that one plus one plus one equals two, say it with conviction. The louder, the better.'

Winging it wasn't Sasha's style. She was more of a fanatical, methodical planner. But it looked like today she'd have a chance to put Noah's method to the test. *Oh, joy.*

32.

ANNABETH DOUGLAS CUPPED HER HANDS around her mug. Leo eyed the seasonal concoction with a distrust that would have made his wife proud—the coffee was mixed with chocolate, pumpkin, whipped cream, and who knew what else. Annabeth seemed to be enjoying it, though, based on her blissful smile.

He raised his own house drip—the Black+Gold, no milk, no sugar—to his mouth and took a drink. He wondered how Sasha's coffee minimalism rubbed off on him without his noticing and suppressed a grin.

"What do you want to know about the Born to Kill trial?" Annabeth asked, absentmindedly petting

Mocha, who had curled up at her feet under the table.

"Everything you can tell me. I read what I could about the gang on-line, but there's not much detail there." As he spoke, he rolled the double stroller back and forth across the porch's uneven plank floor in a rhythm intended to keep the napping twins asleep.

She tapped a finger along her jawline between her chin and her ear as she thought. "Okay. Born to Kill started as a New York street gang made up of young Vietnamese men in the early- to mid-1980s. From what I understand, after the Fall of Saigon, some Vietnamese teenagers made it safely to the United States in the late 1970s. They were scattered throughout the country, but by 1980 or so they somehow congregated in New York, where they briefly fell in with the Flying Dragons."

"That's a Chinese gang, right?"

She nodded. "The Vietnamese guys were pretty tough, so they worked mainly as enforcers for the Flying Dragons for a while. A guy by the name of David Thai left the Flying Dragons, taking along a cadre of Vietnamese gangsters and forming his own gang. They originally called themselves the Canal Boys because their territory was Canal Street. They're largely responsible for establishing Canal Street's flourishing counterfeit market. But by the late 80s, they were calling themselves Born to Kill."

"Any idea where the name originated?" Leo asked, although he already knew from his research. Early in an interview, he found it helpful to establish a conversational rhythm. An effective way to do so was to let the witness talk at length about background information.

"Apparently, 'Born to Kill' was a phrase some American soldiers wrote on their M-1 helmets during the Vietnam War. The gang adopted it, and I have to say it was fitting. Born to Kill was, for several bloody years, the most violent of Chinatown's Asian gangs. Gang members got distinctive tattoos featuring the letters 'B.T.K.,' which, as you might imagine stood for 'Born to Kill.'"

"These tattoos, did they also have a coffin and candles?" Leo leaned forward, eager to hear her answer.

"Right. Three candles. The coffin and candles were supposed to signify that the gang members had no fear of dying." She shivered involuntarily. "It's been years, but I can remember them sitting in that courtroom, hard-eyed and cold. They were completely devoid of remorse or, really, any emotion."

That sounded like dear old dad, all right.

"The gang spread into other areas of the country that had good-sized Vietnamese immigrant populations—as far away as California, Texas, and the southeast. I believe they were even in Canada. They were big into prostitution and drug trafficking everywhere they operated, but they were especially active and violent in New York. They had a protracted turf war with the Ghost Shadows, another Chinatown gang, and were responsible for more than a few rapes and murders, including some murders for hire."

"Tell me about the trial."

"There were actually three big trials. I covered the third one. First, David Thai was arrested. Then the following year, the feds took down the first tier of leaders on racketeering charges."

Now they were getting to the information he needed. "And the third?"

"After the leadership went to prison, B.T.K. was in disarray. There were still drug dealers, foot soldiers, and contract killers running around New York, committing crimes in the gang's name. But no one was in charge. A handful of, well, mid-level managers, I guess, promoted themselves and took over. You had Vien Tran, who was a bookkeeper and managed the bootlegging. Quan Le, who was largely involved in the heroin trade. And then there was Duc Nguyen." She stopped talking and stared down at her drink.

"What did he do?" Leo prompted her.

"Nguyen was an enforcer and a contract killer," she answered slowly. "He racked up quite a body count during his time in B.T.K. When those three took over, they just ramped up the violence. It was a long couple of years for Chinatown. But in 1994, Tran, Le, and Nguyen were arrested and went to trial. I covered it from start to finish. The prosecution had wiretaps, live recordings, ballistics, mutilated corpses, eyewitnesses. They nailed them to the wall."

"But they were never sentenced, were they?"

She shook her head. "The jury came back in less than an hour. Convictions for all three. But, on the sentencing date, the prison van transporting them back to court was ambushed and fire bombed on a deserted stretch of highway outside the city. All three prisoners, as well as the guards and driver, were basically incinerated. Ghost Shadows claimed credit, but so did Flying Dragons. That, in turn, set off a war between the two Chinese gangs, and law enforcement focused on trying to quell that. No one ever closed the loop on the van ambush. I guess the thinking was that it didn't really matter—the three men were off the street and B.T.K. sort of limped along as a minor player after that." She let out a long breath and then inhaled, as if she were trying to use the crisp autumn air to cleanse herself of unpleasant memories.

Leo nodded to himself. Hank, as one would expect, had limited his searches to living people. Faking your death was a time-honored way to give yourself a new life.

After a long, quiet moment, she lifted her coffee cup to her mouth and pasted on a too-bright smile. "So, what's this about a scoop?"

33.

JUDGE NOLAN WAS NOT AMUSED. Sasha didn't know the woman particularly well, but then one didn't need to be the judge's closest gal pal or an expert in psychology to tell that she was pissed.

The judge loomed over her desk and stared directly at Sasha. She forced herself to meet the judge's blazing eyes and not to shrink back in her chair.

"Let me see if I have this straight, Ms. McCandless-Connelly. Your client died yesterday and has already been buried, but instead of having the decency to call my deputy clerk and let us know so we could dissolve the order, you made Mr. Martinello traipse down here from the university for a pointless hearing on a moot point? Not only is this behavior inconsiderate in the extreme, it's a waste of judicial resorts—in other words, my time. And now you tell us your witness is a no-show?"

From the other side of the judge's chambers, George Martinello smirked at her. She ignored her adversary and focused on responding to the tongue-lashing.

"Respectfully, Your Honor, the issue isn't mooted by Mrs. Chevitz's death. There's a real need to protect the patients at Golden Village. In fact, we plan to ask this court to extend and expand the TRO."

Beside her, she saw Naya bracing herself for another explosion. At least the judge had ordered them into chambers so she could berate them off the record rather than in open court, Sasha told herself, trying to find a silver lining.

Martinello scoffed. "Oh, come on. Your Honor, she can't be serious. The order prohibited Dr. Allstrom from harvesting Adina Chevitz's brain tissue. The woman's in the ground now. It's not as if Dr. Allstrom's going to dig her up. This is ridiculous."

Either the university's attorney had seriously poor listening skills or he was deliberately misconstruing what Sasha had just said.

"I'd like to clarify my position for Mr. Martinello, Your Honor. He seems to be confused. We'd

like to seek the extension of the temporary restraining order not to protect Mrs. Chevitz's rights
at this point. The order's necessary to protect *living*
residents of the facility. Dr. Allstrom has engaged
in a pattern and practice of performing medical research without first obtaining informed consent.
That's a violation of federal regulation. And she's
given no indication that she plans to stop. The *only*
reason she didn't take a sample of Mrs. Chevitz's
brain was that the TRO was in place. Unless and
until either the institutional review board or
Golden Village holds her feet to the fire and forces
her to comply with the law, this court is the only
one with the power to prevent her abuses." Sasha
didn't so much as glance in Martinello's direction;
instead, she kept her eyes locked on the judge.

"Is this true, Mr. Martinello? Is your doctor a
cowboy?" Judge Nolan turned her anger on the
other attorney.

He took his time answering. "Why don't we go
ask her, judge? *My* witness did bother to show up.
So I'd rather you hear it from her."

The pointed reference to Dr. Kayser's absence
rankled Sasha. She really hoped that when they
went back to the courtroom, he'd be sitting in the
gallery, appropriately contrite.

The judge stood. Sasha, Naya, and Martinello
leapt to their feet, as well.

After retrieving her robe from the coat rack in the corner of her office, she shook out the wrinkles and pulled it over her head.

"Well, let's do this," she snapped as she pointed them to the door. Sasha and Naya trailed Martinello out of her chambers and down the corridor to the courtroom. Naya reached into her bag and discretely checked her cell phone.

"Any word?" Sasha asked in a low voice so that Martinello wouldn't overhear her. She'd peeked at hers in the judge's chambers; Dr. Kayser hadn't tried to contact her. Maybe he'd called Naya.

Naya shook her head.

Martinello held the door open for them, and they walked into the courtroom. Sasha scanned the empty rows expectantly. Nope. No Dr. Kayser.

Sid Craighead, the judge's affable deputy clerk; the court reporter; and Greta Allstrom all turned to watch them come in. Sid nodded in greeting as they took their places at counsel's table, then he hustled through the door that led directly into the judge's chambers to confer with his boss before she made her entrance.

As soon as the door closed behind him, Naya tugged on Sasha's jacket sleeve. "Does Dr. Allstrom look sick to you?"

Sasha glanced over at the doctor, who was deep in conversation with Martinello. Now that Naya mentioned it, Allstrom did have a distinctly green pallor. And her face looked waxy, as if she'd been sweating.

"Nerves, maybe?" Sasha whispered back.

Naya shrugged.

As if she knew they were talking about her, Greta Allstrom looked over at them. Her pupils were dilated and her eyes darted rapidly from side to side. She didn't look nervous—she looked terrified.

Perfect. She just had to keep Allstrom off-balance and defensive when she took the stand.

The judge's private door opened, and Sid reemerged.

"All stand," he intoned. "The Honorable Pamela Nolan presiding."

The assembled cast popped to their feet as the judge swept into the room like royalty.

"Be seated," Sid instructed them after the judge had arranged herself on the bench.

Judge Nolan smiled at the court reporter. "Ready to go on the record, Emily?"

"Ready when you are, judge."

The judge peered down at Sasha from the bench. "Ms. McCandless-Connelly, it's your party."

Sasha and Naya rose to their feet simultaneously.

"Thank you, Your Honor," Sasha said. She paused. Ordinarily, her next sentence—any attorney's next sentence—would be to identify her client for the record. But seeing as how she didn't technically *have* a client, she squared her shoulders and veered off script. "Your Honor, we're here today because Dr. Greta Allstrom must be stopped."

She could feel Naya staring at her—whether in horror or amazement, she didn't want to know. She plowed forward. "The late Adina Chevitz was forced to spend her final hours on this earth securing an emergency TRO to enjoin Dr. Allstrom from violating her religious beliefs. A dying woman, unable to focus on saying her goodbyes to her family, all because of the arrogance of one doctor. A doctor who is unapologetic about her behavior. A doctor who knowingly, willfully violates best practices regarding informed consent. A doctor who has little, if any, apparent respect for the men and women who have generously enrolled in her research study to aid science."

In her peripheral vision, she saw Martinello struggling not to interrupt her. Allstrom was glaring at her.

The judge held up a hand as if she were a crossing guard. "Hang on. Let's get to the meat of the order, shall we?" She held a copy of the TRO at arm's length and squinted down at the print. "I issued an order that prohibited Dr. Allstrom from interfering in any way with the prompt burial of the body of Adina Chevitz in compliance with Jewish law; specifically, I enjoined the doctor from causing any part of Mrs. Chevitz's body, including, but not limited to, her brain tissue to be autopsied, biopsied, or sampled. And so on and so forth. Correct?"

"Yes, your honor."

"Now, as I understand it, Mrs. Chevitz's agreed to take part in Dr. Allstrom's research study but at the end of her life she reconsidered because of her religious beliefs. I mean, this is a matter of a person, facing death, who changed her mind and revoked her consent. Yes?" The judge shifted her gaze to Martinello.

"Yes," he answered.

"No," Sasha said at the same time.

"Well, which one is it? Yes or no?" The judge practically snarled.

Martinello gave Sasha a sidelong look and then said, "Well, Mrs. Chevitz enrolled in a dementia study and signed an informed consent document agreeing to participate in Dr. Allstrom's research. Now, when she was alive, her participation involved providing periodic blood samples. As Ms. McCandless-Connelly undoubtedly knows, the

Common Rule, as codified within the Code of Federal Regulations protects *living* human study participants. The Common Rule does not apply to tissues obtained post-mortem."

The judge shook her head in frustration. "What are you trying to say, Mr. Martinello? Try it again—in English, please."

"It's complicated, your honor. To the extent Mrs. Chevitz's consent was required, Dr. Allstrom had it. It's not at all clear that she needed consent to harvest post-mortem tissues, but since that activity did conflict with Mrs. Chevitz's Jewish faith, no brain tissue sample was collected. This is a non-issue, frankly."

"Wait just a minute. The reason her brain tissue wasn't sampled was *because* I'd entered an order prohibiting the autopsy. Right?"

"I can't answer that."

"I can, your honor," Sasha volunteered. "It's beyond dispute that Dr. Allstrom knew taking brain tissue was against Mrs. Chevitz's wishes because her personal physician told Dr. Allstrom as much. In addition, there's also no question that Dr. Allstrom fully intended to harvest Mrs. Chevitz's brain tissue *notwithstanding* that fact. Dr. Allstrom instructed a graduate student to go into the lab early on Saturday morning to wait for the brain tissue to arrive."

Sasha paused because Allstrom and Martinello were engaged in a furious whisper fight.

"Counsel, that's enough," the judge barked. "Zip it."

Attorney and client both zipped it, and the judge nodded to Sasha, "Go on, Ms. McCandless-Connelly."

"So while the narrow issue covered by the TRO may be moot, the larger issue remains: Dr. Allstrom doesn't seem to believe she needs consent to perform post-mortem brain autopsies *and* she's willing to go forward with one even when she has actual knowledge that the patient in question *would not consent.* This is abhorrent. It cannot stand. So, we'd like the court to extend the existing restraining order to permanently cover every research participant enrolled in Dr. Allstrom's study."

"You want me to make the order permanent?" the judge echoed.

"Either that or order Dr. Allstrom to go back to each participant and explain the brain tissue harvesting and obtain a second, specific informed consent."

Martinello interrupted, "Your honor—"

"Let me finish, counselor. First of all, I don't think Dr. Allstrom's reading of the Common Rule is a fair one." Sasha gestured toward Naya, who somehow anticipated what she needed and pressed a copy of the CFR into her hands. "The regulations make clear that the key element in the informed consent process is transparency. Study participants must be adequately informed and must be given specific, detailed information. In this case, transparency demands that each prospective patient be told that, depending on the results of their blood tests, there may be a need or desire to take post-mortem brain tissue specimens. Dr. Allstrom didn't do so. It may well be true that the Common Rule doesn't cover specimens obtained post-mortem, but the Uniform Anatomical Gift Act does. Dr. Allstrom didn't limit herself to specimens donated under the UAGA. No, she enrolled living patients in a study, obtained consent for the first portion of her work without telling them her ultimate goal, and then waited for them to die. That's not acceptable."

"I agree with you there, Ms. McCandless-Connelly. But presumably this research is important and in the public good, right?"

"Absolutely!" Martinello interjected. "Dr. Allstrom will be happy to testify as to the extremely beneficial anti-dementia supplement she's created. In addition, if Ms. McCandless-Connelly would kindly stop interfering, the doctor is poised to take her research to the next level. She's close to a breakthrough that would enable dementia sufferers to undergo a cutting-edge procedure to have the supplements applied directly to the myelin sheath via nano-robotic delivery. It's an amazing advance. And the only hurdle left to clear is the study of brain tissue taken from people such as Mrs. Chevitz." He took a moment to turn and glare at Sasha for effect.

"Dr. Allstrom," the judge addressed her directly, "isn't the simplest solution here to simply go back to the subjects and explain the next phase? Those who wish to consent can sign supplemental in-formed consent papers now, and then there's no question as to whether you're complying with the spirit of the law?"

"Well, your honor, that's problematic," Allstrom stammered.

The judge arched an eyebrow and waited. All-strom turned to her attorney.

"Going back to the subjects now could raise more questions than it answers," he said.

"How so?"

Martinello cleared his throat. "Some of the sub-jects have advanced dementia, judge. They don't recognize their kids or know what year it is. If they were to sign off on a brain autopsy, an industrious attorney such as Ms. McCandless-Connelly over there will just come into court and claim they lacked the ability to consent."

Sasha would have bristled at his tone, but the substance was true, so instead she agreed. "I might. But that's no excuse to circumvent the informed consent process. It doesn't exist for the researcher's convenience; it exists for the subject's protection."

Judge Nolan now appeared to be equally irritated with both sides. "I'm inclined to extend this order, but I'm not making it permanent. Ms. McCandless-Connelly, you have three days to get me some actual statistics—how many people are affected by this? Of the enrolled patients, how many have confirmed dementia diagnoses? How advanced are they?"

Naya was scribbling furiously, taking down the directions.

"Yes, your honor."

"Mr. Martinello, your client is to halt all brain tissue harvesting for seventy-two hours. Is that clear, Dr. Allstrom?"

Allstrom's skin was so pale she was almost translucent. Her hands shook, but she nodded her understanding. "Yes, your honor."

"One more thing, Ms. McCandless-Connelly. Don't you dare show up here without a witness on Thursday."

34.

AL KAYSER TURNED HIS HEAD gingerly, first to his left, then to his right, testing his range of motion. His neck was sore and stiff, but the pain in his skull had begun to subside. He tried to lift his hand to probe the lump on his temple but the restraint held taut. He'd forgotten he was tied down.

He stopped struggling and surveyed the room. Judging by the light leaking in around the edges of the blinds it was late morning—at least four hours had passed since he'd been attacked.

It had happened so quickly. He'd parked his old Volvo wagon in Golden Village's staff parking lot, back behind the cottages, leaving the more convenient visitors' spots open for any family members who might be coming to spend time with a resident. His plan had been to pay a quick visit to Mr. Chester before heading into his office to catch up on paperwork for an hour or so before meeting Sasha and Naya at their office. As plans went, it was a fine one.

Davis Chester and Adina Chevitz had been next-door neighbors in the independent living cottages before Adina had transferred to the main building for her final weeks. Davis, a retired florist and an avowed atheist, and Adina had forged a close friendship despite their disparate backgrounds. They shared a love for jigsaw puzzles and had been working on a five-thousand-piece beast of a puzzle, a landscape of a coastal lighthouse, when Adina had started having trouble breathing.

Al had been the one to break the news to Davis. Adina's persistent cough and worsening shortness of breath were signs of pneumonia. Davis had looked at him over his half-moon glasses with a hopeful expression. "Once her lungs clear, she'll move back into her place, though, right?" he'd asked.

Al hadn't made any promises, and, despite Davis's optimism, the man had been at Golden Village long enough to know that trips to the nursing care facility were almost always one-way tickets. In fact, the cottage residents privately referred to the main building as The Hotel California for that very reason.

He'd stopped by yesterday to tell Davis that Adina had passed away. The depth of the man's sadness had taken him by surprise. Most of Al's patients had reached the season of life where the death of a friend was the rule, not the exception. Just as young adults go through a phase when all their friends seem to be getting married, Al's patients—particularly those who lived in community arrangements such as Golden Village—attended a lot of funerals. Death in a retirement home was just a fact of life.

But Davis's grief had been powerful. Al had sat with him for nearly an hour. They'd completed the entire lower left corner of the puzzle while trading stories about Adina. When he'd left, Davis had looked at him with heavy eyes and said, "Will you come tomorrow?"

And so he had.

He'd been crossing the path between Davis's unit and Adina's now-vacant one when footsteps sounded in the gravel behind him. He turned, expecting to see a personal care aide juggling an armload of linens or a janitor hauling a mop and bucket. Instead he found himself staring into a massive barrel chest. He'd had time to register that the chest belonged to a mountain of a man, nearly a full foot taller than he, before the blow to his head dazed him. He wobbled on his feet. The man caught him and carried him across his arms to Adina's unit as if Al were a child, not a one-hundred-and-eighty-pound adult.

Now, as he lay in the hospital bed, each arm tied to a side rail, he felt more rage than fear. He was angry with himself for being so easily overpowered. And he was angry with his enormous captor, whomever he was, for causing him to miss the hearing. That's not to say that he was *unafraid*. He was anxious, to be sure. And worried. But the surprise attack had an absurd quality to it that made his situation seem unreal.

Reality hit him squarely when the man returned. His heavy shoes struck the metal steps outside in a loud, rapid staccato burst.

Al turned to face the door as it opened inward, and the man ushered a slight, white-coated woman into the room. Then the man crossed the threshold and snicked the door lock into place.

Al stared in amazement at Dr. Allstrom.

"What are you thinking?" he demanded.

She gaped back at him, white-faced with fear. "I ... what's going on?" She wheeled around to the hulking man behind her. "Derrick? What's this about?"

"You called the fund. You asked for help. Well, now you got it." He squinted, hard-eyed, at her and then gestured toward the bed where Al was trussed up. "You need a control brain, right? An aging person with no signs of dementia?"

"That's correct? But, what's that have to do with Dr. Kayser?"

Derrick shook his head. "They said you were slow on the uptake. This doctor has been interfering with your research, hasn't he?"

She hesitated. "I guess so. But holding him hostage won't solve anything. The judge extended the restraining order. I can't—"

"Look, lady, there's more than one way to skin a cat. And more than one way to slice a brain."

"I don't follow you."

Al did. *They*—whoever they were—had decided to help Dr. Allstrom's research along by delivering up a healthy brain: his.

As his heart thumped in his chest, comprehension flooded Dr. Allstrom's face.

"Oh, no. No," she moaned.

35.

LEO SAID HIS GOODBYES TO Annabeth and drove home on autopilot. His conversation with her had confirmed his worst fears about Duc Nguyen. His father was a murderous gangster who'd escaped justice. And now Leo knew what he had to do next.

At a red light, he dug out the telephone number his father had given him and activated the Bluetooth. As Doug Wynn's telephone rang, Leo focused on keeping his breathing even.

"Yes? Hello?" Wynn sounded older and weaker than he had just a week earlier.

"It's Leo."

"Yes?" he said in a neutral, mildly interested voice.

Leo had to give grudging respect to the man. He wasn't going to grovel or beg, no matter what.

"I've been doing some research. And I've been thinking."

"And?"

"And I'm willing to make the donation if the hospital here in Pittsburgh accepts you as a patient and clears me as a donor." He glanced down and realized he was gripping the steering wheel so hard that his blue-green veins were protruding from the skin on the underside of his wrists. He relaxed his hold.

"That's not a problem. My doctor has already been in contact with the UPMC transplant program. We assumed that if you agreed, it would be best to have the surgery where you live."

"Oh." Leo said, mainly because he didn't know what else to say.

"I think you should call the donor coordinator and let her know. Her name is Angeline. I have the number here somewhere."

Leo listened to the sound of papers shuffling for a moment then said, "I can find it on the internet."

"Very good."

The prosaic conversation was completely at odds with the emotions coursing through Leo's body. He'd never understood when someone had described an event as being 'surreal,' but now suddenly he did. He concentrated on keeping the SUV on the road.

"Okay, well, I guess I'll let you know what the transplant program says. Or they'll contact your doctor. I'm not sure how it works, to be honest." Leo realized he was babbling.

"It will work out. Leonard?"

"Yes."

Doug Wynn paused for a moment. Leo could hear him breathing, ragged and shallow, on the other end of the phone. Then he said, "Thank you, son."

~ ~ ~ ~ ~ ~ ~ ~ ~ ~

"You did what?" Sasha held the phone away from her ear for a moment and inspected the handset as if it were somehow responsible for the words Connelly had just uttered.

"Sasha—"

"You agreed? You called your father and said, yes, sure, you can have my liver. Why would I want to involve my wife in this sort of decision?"

"I get that you're mad," he said in an evident attempt to stem the tide of anger in her voice.

"*Do* you? Then do you want to explain why you did this? Why did you commit to having the surgery without at least *telling* me first?"

She couldn't fathom why he'd called her in the middle of the workday and dropped this bomb in her lap. She took three deep breaths—cleansing, centering breaths, as her yoga friends would say. Afterwards, she felt oxygenated but no less irate.

"Listen, okay? All I've agreed to at this point is to begin the process. That's it. If he comes here and the doctors at UPMC say he's a good candidate for the surgery *and* the transplant team says I'm a qualified donor, then I'll have to make a final decision. There are a lot of hurdles to clear before I'm lying on the operating table. I just ... I didn't want him to die while I was trying to decide what to do. I don't want that on my conscience, Sasha." He finished in a soft voice.

Her anger deflated. "Okay, that's fair," she conceded. "But I don't have to like it."

"No, you don't."

"Does this mean Hank came through with information about Duc Nguyen's background that gives you comfort?"

Leo was silent for a moment then he said, "Not exactly. It's a long story, but let's just say I found out what I needed to know. I can fill you in some other time."

That struck her as a strange non-answer. She might have probed the subject further, but just then Naya pushed open her door and said, "Dr. Kayser's on hold. Do you want to take it or should Caroline transfer him to my line?"

"Hey, my MIA witness just materialized. I have to go," Sasha said to Connelly, holding up a finger to ask Naya to wait.

"I love you."

"I love you more." She ended the call and looked at Naya, "Come on in. We'll put him on speaker. This better be good."

Naya pulled the door closed behind her and flopped into the nearest chair while Sasha pressed the button to pick up Dr. Kayser's call.

"Dr. Kayser? This is Sasha. I'm putting you on speakerphone because Naya's here, too," she said.

"That's fine. Hello, Naya." His voice sounded scratchy and forced.

"What happened this morning? Where were you?" Sasha asked.

"I came down with something. Perhaps the flu."

Naya tilted her head and gave Sasha a confused look as if to say 'he was too sick to call and let us know?' Sasha nodded. The explanation was wholly unsatisfying.

"We were worried about you. And I'm sorry to hear that you're not feeling well, but the judge was very unhappy. It would have been nice if I'd been able to tell her you were ill."

"I apologize. I was … indisposed."

Sasha waited but he didn't elaborate. She considered that maybe she didn't want to know the details. "Okay, well, take care of yourself and get better as quickly as you can, please. We scored a temporary victory. Judge Nolan did extend the restraining order, but she's scheduled a hearing for Thursday. We need to provide her with specific information—how many people are enrolled in the study, how many are currently diagnosed as having symptoms of dementia. We have a good bit of work to do over the next few days."

He coughed. "I don't think you should count on me for the data or for the hearing, for that matter."

Naya leaned toward the phone and projected her voice. "Dr. Kayser, you aren't serious, are you? We need your help. Your patients need your help."

"I understand but it's beyond my control. Maybe Doctor Craybill can help you?"

"Dr. Craybill?" Naya parroted.

The sound of metal scraping across a wood floor and then muffled voices filtered through the microphone. After a moment, Dr. Kayser spoke again in a strained, nearly unrecognizable voice. "I have to go."

A loud click signified the end of the call.

Sasha and Naya looked at each other in silence. Naya pulled her hands through her short hair. "What in the ever-loving name of Caesar's ghost was that about?"

"Caesar's ghost?" Sasha couldn't resist asking.

Naya tossed her head impatiently. "Carl says it whenever the Steelers fumble. Can we focus here? Who the devil is Dr. Craybill?"

Sasha shrugged. "Your guess is as good as mine. He doesn't have a partner in his practice. And the only Craybill I know is a former client up in Firetown ..." She trailed off and rubbed her eyes.

"What is it?"

"Jed Craybill isn't a doctor. Judge Paulson appointed me to represent him."

"That whole hydrofracking mess?" Naya asked. The scandal had predated Naya's time at the firm, but she'd heard plenty about the Clear Brook County shenanigans.

"Right. Mr. Craybill's doctor declared him incompetent, but he wasn't. I asked Dr. Kayser to evaluate him and testify on his behalf at the incapacitation hearing." Sasha spoke slowly, trying to shape the ideas in her mind into some semblance of sense.

Naya's face mirrored the confusion Sasha felt. "What does it mean? Why'd he bring up that case?"

"It could be a coincidence. Maybe there *is* a Dr. Craybill who could help us. We can ask his receptionist." Sasha couldn't ignore the way her pulse fluttered in her throat. "Or," she continued, "maybe it's a message."

"What do you mean—a message?"

"He could be trying to tell us something. Something he couldn't just come out and say for some reason."

"Like what?" Naya demanded.

Sasha's stomach tightened. "I don't know, but I'm sure it's nothing good."

~ ~ ~ ~ ~ ~ ~ ~ ~ ~

Al blinked innocently at his captors. "How was that?"

"Nobody asked you to ad lib, doc," Derrick said as he popped his knuckles.

"It was fine. You did fine," Dr. Allstrom hurried to assure him.

He'd done what he could. Sasha would either realize that something was terribly wrong or she wouldn't. All that was left to do now was to pray.

Derrick said, "Come on, Dr. Allstrom. I'll walk you to your car."

"W-w-wait," she stammered.

He turned and stared at her stone-faced. "What is it?"

"His brain. I can't use it if I haven't already analyzed his blood markers. I need to take samples, run them through the centrifuge, and plot the results."

Al watched her face closely—was she trying to buy him time or just make sure that when this hulking behemoth of a man killed him it advanced her research goals? He couldn't tell.

Judging by the cloud of confusion that crossed Derrick's face, he wasn't sure either. "How long's that going to take?"

Allstrom bobbed her head back and forth like a metronome while she thought. "I can put a rush on the blood analysis. Two days, probably."

Derrick began to huff out an objection but Allstrom drew herself to her full height and cut him off. "I beg your pardon, but this is *my* project. If the Alpha Fund wants to realize a return on its investment, you'll need to respect the process, not interfere with it."

He crossed his arms and narrowed his eyes into slits. "Go get your blood draw equipment and hurry back. I'll babysit him until Thursday morning, no longer. Are we clear?"

Allstrom didn't answer. She was already scurrying out of the cottage.

Derrick nodded at him. "Looks like you got a reprieve. You gotta use the john?"

36.

Monday Evening

EVENTS BEGAN TO BLUR. As soon as Doug Wynn called the oncologist's office to say that his son had agreed to donate his liver, some unseen, dormant machinery sprang to life.

Less than two hours after the call, a medical helicopter was landing in his backyard. He was bundled on to a stretcher and loaded into the aircraft— a private medical escort service that he was more than happy to pay for. By the time the sun was setting, he was being whisked through a private underground corridor normally reserved for Middle Eastern sheiks and royalty and then settled into his bed on the transplant ward in the University of Pittsburgh Medical Center hospital in Oakland. Blood was drawn, his temperature taken, his abdomen scanned.

A collage of cheerful female faces whirred by. Becky, his aide; Charlene, his nurse; Valerie, the resident. Every one of them asking the same litany of questions as she rubbed hand sanitizer between her palms. Do you have any concerns? Do you understand what's happening? Are you in pain?

He answered everyone in halting English. Which was odd because he'd adopted the language wholeheartedly. He even dreamed in English.

He was watching 'The Big Bang Theory' on the ceiling-mounted television with the sound off, when Lester Baker, the surgeon who would be performing the surgery—if it happened—strolled into the room.

"Mr. Wynn," he said cheerfully. "How are we tonight?"

"I'm fine. And you, doctor?"

"We're getting up to speed on your charts. You're a very sick man, Mr. Wynn."

"Please, call me Doug."

"Doug, your tumors are just barely within the acceptable parameter of a Milan score. If we're going to do this, we need to jam."

"To jam?" he repeated uncertainly.

"To move quickly. Forge ahead. We're calling your son in for his evaluation tomorrow. We'll be putting a rush on the whole thing. Seems you're on the Arabian King Plan, eh?"

"I beg your pardon?"

"Foreign dignitaries. Rich men from other countries. They show up, no insurance, pay cash for everything. It certainly expedites the process, not having to go round and round with medical insurance bean counters, eh?"

"Heh." Doug laughed weakly. He didn't want to invite any questions about his finances. He had gobs of money, to be sure. The means by which he'd acquired those sums would not withstand close scrutiny, as his accountant used to say.

"That's a good thing, Mr. Wynn. That means that if your son's a match, you could have your surgery as early as this week."

"Really?" Doug coughed and raised himself onto his elbows. That was sooner than he had allowed himself to hope.

Dr. Baker reached out and patted him on the shoulder. "Let's not get ahead of ourselves. Leo is coming in tomorrow. We'll know by the end of the day."

37.

Tuesday

"THANKS, MOM," Sasha kissed Valentina on the cheek and waved goodbye to her dad.

"Honey, truly, any time," her dad assured her as he hefted the groaning bag stuffed full of baby supplies on to the kitchen counter.

"We really appreciate it," Connelly said soberly.

"Leo, please. It's such an amazing thing you're doing. Just amazing. Saving a life—your father's life!" Her mom teared up at the thought.

Sasha planted a kiss on Fiona's forehead and then one on Finn's before grabbing Connelly's hand and hurrying him through her parent's kitchen door and out to the waiting car.

She buckled her seatbelt, adjusted her side mirrors, started the engine, and then glanced over at her passenger. "You okay?"

"Fine."

"Are you sure? You're quiet."

He stared straight ahead as he answered. "I really didn't expect things to happen this quickly."

Quickly was, in her view, a bit of an understatement. Less than eighteen hours ago, he'd decided to move forward with the possibility—the *possibility*—of donating part of his liver to his father. And somehow, now, his father was already checked in at the hospital in Oakland and had been cleared for a living donor donation. The only missing piece of this puzzle? Connelly.

But as she watched that muscle twitch in his jaw, she felt only sympathy. No snark. No blame. Just the sinking feeling of knowing how it felt to carry the weight of someone else's existence on your shoulders.

She dug back through her memory to the night she'd gone into labor to find an approximation of the words Connelly had used. "This is it. Are you ready?"

They must have resonated, because he squeezed her hand then raised it to his lips for a kiss. "I'm ready," he said pinning his clear gray eyes on hers.

"Let's do this, then," she said as she hit the gas pedal and the car lurched forward out of the alley.

She spent the short drive down the hill into town reminding herself that her role here was to be supportive. She wondered how Connelly had managed to stay so calm when she'd been about to give birth with the twins. Here she was, just driving him to an intake appointment, and her hands were so shaky she nearly hit the guardrail as she merged onto Bigelow Boulevard.

She passed a billboard advertising Golden Village's superior, aging population solutions and made a mental note to call Dr. Kayser's office to see whether anyone there knew a Dr. Craybill. By the time she pulled into the parking garage behind Montefiore Hospital, she'd forgotten all about Dr. Kayser's cryptic message.

~ ~ ~ ~ ~ ~ ~ ~ ~ ~

"Tomorrow?" Leo repeated, certain that he'd misheard the woman. The walls seemed to close in on him. The air was heavy and hot. His throat felt as if it were closing. He focused on taking the next breath.

"That's right," Angeline chirped. "Isn't that amazing? You just *flew* through the health and mental screenings. And it's clear you have family support." She paused here to smile at Sasha, who squeezed his hand so tightly he was sure she crushed a few of his fingers.

"What about scheduling an operating room and a surgical team? People are just sitting around waiting for a surgery?" Sasha asked.

"That's another stroke of good luck. Dr. Bryant, who will be performing Leo's surgery, does all of his surgeries on Wednesdays. This Wednesday, as it happens, he didn't have a surgery scheduled. Dr. Baker, who will be operating on Mr. Wynn is also free in the morning. And because Mr. Wynn is a cash patient we didn't need to go through the process of submitting anything to his insurance—"

"He's paying cash for a liver transplant?" Leo asked.

"Yep. And he's picking up the cost of your surgery, too."

"Excuse me?"

"Typically, the recipient's insurance covers the donor's surgery and follow-up, too. Because your father doesn't have insurance we ordinarily would have checked with your insurer to see if they'd cover you, but he told us not to. He's going to go out of pocket for the entire amount." Angeline smiled broadly.

"Where would your dad get that kind of money?" Sasha asked out of the side of her mouth.

Blood money, he thought. "No idea," he said.

"So, Leo, the question for you is whether you'd like us to find you a room or if you want to spend the night at home and come back early tomorrow morning?"

He turned to Sasha. She gripped her fistful of glossy full-color brochures and looked at him wide eyed. He knew exactly what she was feeling. He also knew he wanted to sleep in his bed next to his wife tonight with her narrow back curved against his chest, his arm tight around her waist, and her wild waves of hair tickling his nose every time she shifted in her sleep.

"I'll come back tomorrow," he said.

"Great. Let me walk you through the pre-op information," Angeline said.

"Excuse me. I'll be back in a bit." Sasha stood and walked out of the room stiffly, as if she were in a trance.

"She's probably a little bit stunned," Angeline suggested, as they watched her go. "It's understandable. It can be a shock to the family when the idea of the transplant suddenly shifts from abstract to imminent. Just give her some time."

38.

SASHA HESITATED OUTSIDE THE DOOR to Doug Wynn's private room. Visiting the father-in-law she'd never met had seemed like a good idea when she'd bolted from the transplant coordinator's office. But now that she'd made her way to the eleventh floor and located his room, it seemed like a strange, potentially awkward thing to do. She was backing away, headed toward the stairwell, when a tall, friendly nurse's aide bustled out of the room, pushing a meal cart, and nearly bumped into her.

"Oh, I'm sorry, honey. I didn't see you there."

"It's okay."

"You can go ahead in. Mr. Wynn's awake," the woman assured her before she disappeared around the corner.

Just do it, already.

She cleared her throat, raised her hand, and gave the door a quick rap with her fist.

"Come in," a male voice called.

She pushed open the door and walked into the room.

Doug Wynn was propped up in his bed with two pillows wedged behind his back. An untouched bowl of cherry Jell-O and a Styrofoam cup filled with water rested on the tray in front of him.

He glanced down from the ceiling-mounted TV screen and met her gaze.

"Do you need something?" He eyed her from head to toe, taking in her tailored dress and jacket, and apparently decided she was there in some sort of official capacity.

For her part, she blocked out the too-loud volume of his sitcom and its canned laugh track; the chill of the stale institutional air that circulated around her; and the faint scent of bleach and disinfectant that hung like a cloud over the sparse room. She focused on the man in the bed. Searched his angular, lined face for a hint of her husband. But there was no trace of Connelly's warmth and wit in this man's hard, dull eyes. No glimmer of the good humor that curved Connelly's full lips into a perpetual bow in Wynn's firm, unyielding frown. She saw nothing that tied the two men together.

Yet, Wynn's blood coursed through Connelly's veins. And, by this time tomorrow, Connelly's liver would be nestled in Wynn's abdomen, already beginning its work, clearing toxins from the sick man's body, pumping health and life back into his dying husk.

He stared back at her in a cold silence that rebuffed her. Then he repeated his question in a flat tone, "Do you need something?"

She stepped closer to his bed. "I'm Sasha McCandless-Connelly," she finally answered in a voice that cracked just a bit. "I wanted to meet you before tomorrow."

His face was a blank mask. "No visitors."

"I'm sorry, maybe you don't recognize my name? I'm Leo's wife. I'm married to your son."

He closed his eyes for a moment. She waited. When he reopened them and saw her still standing there, he raised his eyebrows slightly as though he were surprised to see that she hadn't taken the hint and vanished. She smiled in an attempt to bridge the awkward distance between them—strangers who at once shared nothing and absolutely everything.

He turned his head and faced the wall.

She took out her phone. "Would you like to see a picture of your grandchildren?" she asked as she swiped through the most recent shots of the twins, looking for one that captured their nascent person-alities.

"No."

She drew back as if he'd slapped her. *No?* The hair on the back of her neck prickled. Her tentative efforts to reach out to the man were forgotten, and anger flared in her belly.

"Well, you need to. Their father—*their* father who's raising them—is risking his life tomorrow to save yours. The least you can do is acknowledge his family."

He turned back and locked eyes with her. His expression was icy. "I told Leonard, and I'm telling you. I want nothing to do with his family. Now, go. Or I'll call the nurse and have you removed."

He dismissed her and shifted away from her in the bed. She stared at his profile for a moment longer—and, in that final instant, she saw it. The barest shadow of Connelly. The muscle in the old man's left cheek was pulsing in silent anger.

She turned and walked out of the room.

39.

GRETA PACED AROUND HER LIVING room in a futile effort to work through her anxiety. Everything was wrong. It was wrong for her to be at home in the middle of the day. It was wrong for her to risk falling further behind in her work. Her pulse raced at the thought of what would happen if she failed to deliver the results the Alpha Fund had paid for.

But she couldn't sit in her office, fielding Virgil's well-intentioned, worried calls and scrolling through the innumerable last-minute instructions that George Martinello was emailing her in periodic bursts as he prepared for the upcoming hearing.

She tried to convince herself that these distractions were upsetting her. But her excuse rang hollow even to her. She was upset by something much worse.

She was hiding in her apartment in an effort to forestall reality. Any minute now, a technician from the phlebotomy lab would upload the results from the 'John Doe' blood analysis. And then she'd be out of time. Dr. Kayser would be out of time.

Her stomach churned. Derrick was going to kill him unless she came up with a way to stop it. On Monday, she'd still had hope that Athena would move a new resident into the empty cottage and discover Dr. Kayser. That hadn't happened.

Then this morning, when Coretta Gardner starting seizing, Greta had allowed herself to hope that the woman would die. Then she'd *have* her healthy brain and would only need George Martinello to convince the court to let her use it. But Coretta's seizures had turned out to be the result of a new medication, and the staff had quickly stabilized her.

Now it was Tuesday afternoon, and as the hours passed, Greta was forcing herself to face the truth: By Thursday, Dr. Kayser would be dead. Unless she did something.

A sob escaped her lips and she began to cry again. She reached for another tissue and wiped her puffy, swollen eyes.

How could she save Dr. Kayser without getting herself killed in the process? Going to the police wasn't option. It would be the equivalent of pulling on a loose thread and unraveling an entire sweater. The specifics of the Alpha Fund investment would come to light. She'd lose her professorship. Her work would be shut down. She'd be arrested. And if, somehow, she didn't end up in prison, she'd spend the rest of her life hiding from the Alpha Fund.

But could she really let Derrick kill Dr. Kayser? The blood would be on her hands, too.

She shredded the tissue into fine pieces that fluttered to the floor as she walked and thought.

Her work was so important, though. If the nano-robotic supplement delivery could prevent age-related cognitive deterioration, she would be improving the quality of life for literally millions of people. She'd be viewed as a hero. Was it even morally right to weigh the life of one man against all the potential good she could do?

The room was spinning. She lowered herself into a chair and breathed through her rising nausea. She had no good options. For that matter, she had precious few *bad* options. And time was slipping away, minute by minute.

40.

"**M**AC, WE THINK YOU SHOULD go home."

Sasha looked up at the sound of Naya's voice. Naya stood just inside Sasha's office door, her arms crossed and her legs planted, as if she were a bouncer just waiting for a fight. Beside her, Caroline was wringing her hands in a nervous gesture. And behind them, loomed her law partner, Will Volmer, whose forehead was so wrinkled with worry that he resembled the pug puppy his wife had gotten him for his birthday.

"You people look a mess," she joked, hoping the words masked the unnatural tremble in her voice.

Ever since she'd left Doug Wynn's hospital room, she'd been keyed up. She was shaky, distracted. Her stomach was tight, her throat dry. But her friends and coworkers looked to be at least as terrified as she was—possibly more so. She let her pen fall to her desk.

"I'm fine, really. I just want to finish up some correspondence and then I'll go home for the night," she reassured them.

"You should go home *now,* spend some time with Leo. Stop trying to be superwoman," Will intoned.

"I appreciate the concern, but really, you guys, I want to tie up as many loose ends as I can now so I don't have to worry about them tomorrow while he's in surgery." She flashed a smile that she suspected was wholly unconvincing.

Naya uncrossed her arms and walked over to Sasha's desk. "Leave the loose ends. Please, go. We'll handle anything that comes up. I promise."

Sasha's eyes filled with tears at the gentle note in her hard-nosed associate's voice. She blinked them away.

"Yes, go home and hug those babies tight," Caroline agreed.

In the distance, Sasha could hear the main telephone line ringing at the reception desk. No one moved to answer it. She looked from Will to Caroline to Naya. They looked back at her somberly. Finally, the phone stopped ringing.

She nodded. "Okay, I hear you. I'm going."

Relief washed over each of their faces.

"Good," Will said. "Susan and I will be praying for Leo and his father." He patted her on the shoulder and turned to leave.

Sasha tried to thank him, but she couldn't find her voice.

Caroline leaned in for a quick hug. "I will, too. Please call us when you can give an update tomorrow, okay?"

"Sure thing," she managed.

Naya waited until Caroline walked away. "You know, I'm gonna stand here until you pack up your little bag and head off into the sunset, right?"

"I sort of figured."

Naya put a hand on her hip in an exaggerated gesture. "So get cracking."

Sasha laughed for the first time in hours and started gathering her belongings as instructed. "Do you think you're up for handling the hearing on Thursday?"

"By myself?"

"By yourself."

"Damn straight I am." Naya's enthusiasm rolled off her in waves.

Sasha nodded. "I figured you'd be excited to do it. You'll have a lot of legwork to do tomorrow. I guess Dr. Kayser's still out sick."

"He is. I meant to tell you. I called his office this morning. Ruth has never heard him mention a Dr. Craybill, and she searched his contacts—nothing there. He did call in and leave a message for her that he was very sick and she should cancel all his appointments for the rest of the week."

"Did she mention whether he said anything cryptic?" Sasha wondered.

"No. I asked. She said he left a voicemail. He sounded tired and strained, but there was no secret message or anything. What do you think's going on?"

"I really can't imagine. Maybe the university reached out to him and worked something out to get him to back off?"

"Then why not just tell us and let the TRO expire? He wouldn't play us like that. Would he?" Naya asked.

"I wouldn't think so, but the whole disappearing act makes no sense. So he has the flu. He's not *dying*. He was so committed to protecting his patients, and now he can't be bothered. There's something really off about this."

Dr. Kayser's behavior rankled her. And it worried her. She wondered if she'd be able to figure out his reason for mentioning Craybill if she were better able to focus. Then she wondered if she might be obsessing over a misspoken word in an effort to distract herself from Connelly's upcoming surgery.

Naya was watching her closely. "You okay?"

"Yeah. This informed consent case makes my brain hurt, that's all."

"Like I said, Mac. Go home."

~ ~ ~ ~ ~ ~ ~ ~ ~ ~

Greta stared at the wall. She'd tried. She'd managed to screw up her courage and had called the McCandless & Volmer law firm. She wasn't exactly sure what she would have said if she'd been able to speak to either Sasha McCandless-Connelly or Naya Andrews, but she would have said *something*, given them some hint about the serious situation Dr. Kayser was in. But no one answered the phone. She'd counted to seventeen rings and then hung up, her palms damp, her heart galloping in her chest.

She was at once relieved that her last-ditch effort had failed and horrified at what it would mean for her and Dr. Kayser. Someone was going to die. And it wasn't going to be Greta Allstrom.

41.

Wednesday Morning

VALENTINA CAUGHT SASHA'S ARM AS she flew through the kitchen on her way to the refrigerator.

"Honey—"

"Hang on, Mom. I just need to get these bottles ready for you and Dad."

"Sasha, stop. Forget about the milk for a minute, okay?"

Something in her mother's voice made her comply. She froze where she stood and turned to face her mom. "What is it?"

"Don't worry about the twins. If they wake up and need you, we'll bring them to the hospital. You focus on your husband. He needs you now." Valentina's eyes were serious.

Her mother leaned in to give her a hug. Sasha found herself clinging to Valentina's shoulders, inhaling the cloud of Happy perfume that hung around her like a curtain. "Okay, Mom. You're right."

Valentina pulled back in mock amazement. "Did you hear that, Pat? Sasha just said I was *right* about something."

Sasha rewarded her with a shaky laugh. "I'm going to run upstairs and see if Connelly's almost ready."

"You should put your hair up," her mother observed, sliding seamlessly from the unfamiliar role of emotional support back to the more familiar ground of constructive critic.

"Mom—"

"And use Nana's hairpin."

Even for Valentina, that was an oddly specific dictate.

"Pardon? You want me to wear the *kanzashi*? Do you know something I don't? Am I going to have to fight my way out of a corner?"

Her mother had given her Nana's antique geisha hairpin, which doubled as a weapon in a pinch. The pin was about six inches long, with a wicked point.

"Don't be silly. I'm not suggesting you need it to protect yourself. Well, actually I guess I am." Her mother's voice grew wistful, and she twisted a tarnished gold ring around on her right thumb.

Sasha forgot about the hair ornament and stared at the ring. "Is that ... Patrick's class ring?" When had her mom started wearing her deceased oldest child's school ring?

"Yes. I wear it when I need to feel Patrick's spirit watching over me. And that's why I'm suggesting you wear your grandmother's hairpin. It has Nana Alexandrov's essence in it. She'll protect Leo."

Sasha cocked her head and studied her mother's face. She appeared to be completely serious.

Over Valentina's shoulder, Sasha's dad caught her eye. He gave her a long, meaningful look that clearly said 'Don't argue with her. Just do it.' She recognized it well, having been on the receiving end approximately five hundred times between the ages of fourteen and eighteen.

"Good idea, Mom," she said and turned to leave, only barely resisting the urge to roll her eyes just as teenaged Sasha would have.

She tiptoed up the stairs so as not to wake Finn and Fiona and eased open the door to the master bedroom. Connelly was fully dressed, sitting on the edge of the bed, staring down at something in his hands—it was the framed black-and-white picture he'd taken of her holding the twins during their first hour of life.

Uh-oh.

She opened her jewelry armoire and pawed through its contents until she found the jeweled pin. Then she twisted her hair into a low knot and jabbed the *kanzashi* through it.

Connelly glanced up.

"Don't ask," she said, gesturing to her hairstyle.

She joined him on the bed and looked down at the picture in his hands.

After a moment she said, "It's hard to believe they were ever that tiny, isn't it?"

He nodded but didn't speak.

"You don't have to do this," she said, knowing as she uttered the words that he would say he did.

"Yes, I do."

She smiled sadly and eased the picture out of his hands, returning it to the bedside table. "I guess you do, because you wouldn't be you otherwise. Are you ready?"

He stood and swept her into a tight embrace. They stood silently, the only sounds their beating hearts, their soft breathing, and the muted tick-tock of the clock on the dresser.

After an eternity, he pulled away and cleared his throat. "We should go." He turned, swiped the photograph off the nightstand, and slipped it into his overnight bag.

~ ~ ~ ~ ~ ~ ~ ~ ~ ~

Sasha wasn't sure how long she'd been sitting in the waiting room. Time slowed to a crawl, every minute suspended in amber like a prehistoric insect preserved for an eternity. The other anxious occupants of the room clustered in small groups, laughing too loudly, talking too much—frenetic energy designed to ward off troubling thoughts. It seemed as though all the other patients had teams of family members and friends hunkered down in the waiting room, cheering on their loved one. At least one had a literal team, with matching t-shirts that read "Hope for Hope."

Connelly had her. And his father had no one. She knew she could have called one of her brothers or their wives to come sit with her. Or Hank. Or Daniel and Chris. Someone would have joined her. But she didn't want to have to talk about the amazing gift Connelly was giving his father. Because that conversation inevitably would lead to a more general conversation about Connelly's long-lost father. And that was a discussion she wanted to avoid.

So she sat off by herself and read a book she'd picked almost at random from the gift shop—or pretended to. After she read the same passage for the fourth time she admitted to herself that in her current state of mind the book was a prop, nothing more.

After three hours, her neck and back were stiff and tight. She considered taking a walk, checked the electronic status board, and saw that both Connelly and Wynn were in surgery. She decided not to leave out of some superstition that as long as she kept the waiting room vigil, they would both be safe.

She used the far corner of the room as a makeshift gym to do some stretches. Then she refilled her coffee and opened her book to a page at random.

Halfway through the fourth hour, her stomach began to growl so loudly that she feared the noise would disturb Team Hope. She rummaged through her bag and pulled out a package of almonds. She ate them one at a time while she stared down at the strings of words on the page. Once she'd eaten the entire bag, she pawed through her bag looking for a napkin or tissue to clean the salt from her fingers.

Instead she found a small cream-colored envelope with a loopy cursive 'S' scrawled across the front.

A note from Connelly.

She opened it with shaking hands:

"The more I give to thee, the more I have, for both are infinite."

That was the entire message—one snippet of a passage from *Romeo and Juliet*. The passage that they'd read to one another during their wedding ceremony. But what did it mean in this context? She closed her eyes and focused and suddenly she knew. His gift to his father was an offering of love. And even if Duc Nguyen never returned it, it would come back to him as more love, infinite love. And, through him, to her and the twins. This was his goodbye, just in case the unimaginable happened. She watched as the letters began to blur and then swim before her eyes.

Then she rested her head on her knees and wept.

She could hear the din of conversation in the room diminish and knew if she raised her head and opened her eyes she'd see dozens of curious, uncertain eyes watching her awkwardly.

Pull it together, she ordered herself. When she was able to look up, Naya and her old neighbor

Maisy were standing over her, looking down with expressions of panic.

"Did somethin' go wrong with the surgery, sugar?" Maisy asked, her syrupy Southern accent filled with fear.

Sasha shook her head and sniffled. "No. I guess I'm just a little emotional. I'm sorry."

Naya's eyebrows shot up to her hairline. "Good gravy, Mac. Don't apologize. Here. From Jake."

Naya handed her a stainless steel travel mug filled with steaming hot coffee. Sasha inhaled. Steel City Nic, her favorite.

"Thanks," she said with a wobbly grin.

"Wait, there's more." Naya reached into her large, leather purse and removed a wrap. "The girls working the counter made you a salmon BLT. Something about omega-3 and mood and, ah, hell, I wasn't listening. They thought it would make you feel better. Looks like you could use a pick-me-up. Although I don't know about fish as a treat."

She took the sandwich and the fistful of napkins that Naya offered and balanced them on her lap.

"Where'd you run into Maisy?" Sasha asked. The surgery had been scheduled so quickly, she hadn't had time to let all of their friends know. Had Maisy been in Oakland just by chance?

"I went down to the television station and got her," Naya said. "It's not healthy for you to sit here all by your lonesome all day. I have to prepare for the hearing or else I'd stay here myself. But, you know, if there's one thing Maisy is, it's a good conversationalist. I figured she can distract you with her single girl tales of dating disasters."

"Well, that's for sure," Sasha agreed. She felt the ghost of a smile forming on her lips.

Maisy's blue eyes danced with laughter. "I can hear y'all. Y'all know that, right?"

Sasha giggled. Naya snorted. And Maisy threw back her mass of big blonde curls and howled with laughter.

Once they'd caught their breath, Naya grew serious. "I do have to go, though, Mac. Athena Ray let me camp out in her office this morning and go through Dr. Kayser's files. I need to get back to the office and organize my notes. I also strong-armed Athena into testifying. She won't add much, but I'm sure as shooting not showing up without someone to put in the witness chair."

Sasha nodded. "Good instincts."

Naya grinned and then suddenly snapped her fingers. "Oh, this is weird. I'm pretty sure Dr. Kayser left his car at Golden Village. There's one that looks just like his parked back by those cottages."

"That doesn't make any sense. What did Athena say about it?"

"I didn't notice until I was on my way out, so I haven't mentioned it to her."

Sasha watched her walk away, wondering what Dr. Kayser was up to.

After a moment, Maisy cleared her throat. "Honey, if you aren't going to eat that wrap, hand it over. I missed lunch today."

42.

Wednesday evening

LEO LOOKED UP INTO HIS wife's bright green eyes and smiled.

"Finally," she said. "You're awake. How do you feel?"

He grimaced. "Like I was hit by a truck."

"Dr. Bryant said you did great. There were no complications. Apparently you had the textbook right liver lobe."

"Sounds sexy. Go on."

She leaned over and brushed his lips with a kiss. "Your father had a rougher time of it. He was bleeding a lot, hemorrhaging, I guess. But Dr. Baker got him stabilized. He's still in the TICU, but he's going to pull through."

He let out a soft sigh of relief at the news, then he said, "Where am I?"

"This is your room. I came down to see you while you were in the TICU, but you were pretty loopy."

"Did I say anything stupid?"

"Of course not. Like what?"

"Oh, like my father is a member of a Vietnamese street gang and a convicted murderer who faked his own death to escape justice? Anything along those lines?"

She stared at him, not comprehending, for a moment. Then her eyes widened. "Are you sure?"

"I'm sure," he said. His lips were dry and cracking. "Can I have some water?"

"Not yet. The nurse said start with ice. Here."

She placed an ice chip from the cup near his bed into his mouth, and he let it melt and run down his throat. The cold liquid was like a glimpse of heaven.

"Ah, thank you."

"Don't mention it. Can we get back to the murderous gangster thing? When did you find out?"

He inhaled deeply then winced. Apparently shallow breaths were the way to go. "Monday."

"Monday?" she echoed. "You found out before you agreed to the transplant?" Her face and voice were very careful, as if she were struggling to maintain her temper.

"Yes." He watched as her face tightened and her cheeks flushed.

"Connelly, how could you?"

"He's my father, Sasha."

She stared down at him with sad, disappointed eyes. He didn't look away.

"Still—" she began.

"Still nothing. I couldn't let him die." He balled his hands into fists, clenched them, then relaxed them. "And I also can't let him get away with murder."

"What are you saying?"

"Is Hank outside?"

"Yes."

"Can you ask him to come in, so I only have to explain this once?" Speaking took more effort than he'd anticipated. And every breath he drew caused a sharp poker of fire to run along his abdomen.

"Sure. Of course." She hurried out into the hallway, stopping in the doorway to look over her shoulder at him with a puzzled expression.

She returned with Hank and Annabeth Douglas.

"Ah, Hank already called you," Leo said in greeting to Annabeth.

"Yes, Mr. Richards tells me it's time to turn in my chip and collect that exclusive story I was promised."

"He's right," Leo said.

"You sure do like to make it dramatic, don't you?" the reporter observed.

Leo cleared his throat. "Well, I wasn't about to let a man die if I could help. But I'm not going to let him evade prosecution any more. Agent Richards has a warrant for the arrest of Duc Than Nyugen, also known as Doug Wynn, a member of the Born to Kill gang convicted of murder and racketeering in 1984 and presumed dead after a firebombing before he could be sentenced. I thought you might like to tag along when Hank takes him into custody."

Leo was addressing Annabeth, but his eyes were pinned on his wife.

Sasha gasped softly.

"You're sure you don't want to wait until your old man is conscious and talk to him one last time before you set this all in motion, son?" Hank asked. "Once you pull this trigger, there's no going back. He's not going anywhere. I've got two guys posted outside his door."

Leo set his mouth in a hard line. He felt the familiar twitch of the muscle that ran from his cheek to his jaw. "I'm sure. I'm done with Duc Nyugen."

Hank nodded. "Get some rest, would you? Come on, Ms. Douglas. I can fill you in on the elevator on our way downstairs."

Annabeth trailed Hank out of the room mutely, and Leo turned to his wife.

"Are you disappointed in me?" he asked, holding his breath while he waited for her answer.

"For what?"

"For turning him in? Or for saving him? Or both?" he countered.

Tears shined in her eyes. She leaned over and cupped his face gently in her hands. "I'm not disappointed. I could never be disappointed in you. I can't imagine how hard this has been for you. To agree to do this knowing what you knew about him."

He shook his head. "It wasn't hard at all. Making a decision with full information is the easiest thing in the world."

43.

Very early Thursday morning, just after midnight

SASHA STRUGGLED TO KEEP HER eyes open as she made her final trip of the impossibly, immeasurably long day. She'd been back and forth between the house and the hospital four times. Leo was resting comfortably. According to her parents, the twins had been asleep for hours. Now it was her turn. She was drained. Exhausted. Done.

Too late, she realized that she'd missed the turn onto Fifth Avenue. She swore softly under her breath. The next several blocks were one way. So she snaked through Oakland and came down

Forbes hill, approaching Shadyside from the far side.

Of course, she got stuck at the traffic light. As she sat, waiting for red to turn to green, on the deserted, sleeping street, she glanced to her left. She realized she was looking at the back of Golden Village. The black wrought-iron fence ran the length of the block, but from this vantage point it just looked like an urban park, lacking the impressive liberal arts campus or monied estate vibe that it projected from the front.

She remembered what Naya had said and squinted at the staff parking spots set back from the cottages. Two cars sat side by side in the two furthest spaces. The one on the right *did* look like Dr. Kayser's, she had to admit.

Just then, the front door of one of the independent living cottages opened and two people, a small-ish woman and a mountain of a man stepped out on to the walk. They speed-walked from the structure to the cars with bowed heads, looking for all the world like two people trying not to be seen.

That's weird. The cottages *were* reserved for residents who could live independently, but it was a bit late for anyone to be receiving visitors. The light turned green. Sasha coasted down the hill several feet, keeping her eyes on her rearview mirror. The woman got into the car parked next to the one that looked like Dr. Kayser's. As she started the engine, her headlights washed over the man, spotlighting him for a few seconds. Long enough for Sasha's spidey senses to start tingling, as her nephews would say.

The man screamed 'enforcer.' Ill-fitting suit that barely contained his body-builder physique. Close-cropped military haircut. He raised a hand as the woman drove past him then jogged back to the cottage he'd come from. Before opening the door, he reached a hand inside his suit jacket, the way one would if one had a gun.

This is all wrong.

She eased forward until she was far enough down the road to have a decent view of the gated exit from the lot then pulled over and put the car in park. She'd get a peek at the side of the woman's face as she pulled out, before she turned.

As it happened, a glimpse of profile was all she needed: Dr. Allstrom zipped out of the parking lot, hunched over her steering wheel, and sped down the empty street.

Sasha turned the key and killed the ignition. *Think it through.*

Dr. Kayser went missing at a critical time for the case. When he finally called, his explanation was ludicrous and he tossed out a seemingly random reference to Jed Craybill. She thought back to the case involving Mr. Craybill. Almost lost among the murders, land transfers, and illicit wheeling and dealing of the local politicians was the fact that Dr. Kayser had figured out that their client was essentially being held captive. His treating physician had been drugging him—using an anticholinergic allergy medication with side effects that mimicked the symptoms of dementia—to convince everyone that the man was, in fact, mentally incapacitated. And now Dr. Allstrom and a large, sketchy-looking man were skulking around in the middle of the night at a place where Dr. Kayser's car just happened to be parked, even though he hadn't been seen in days.

Sasha took the keys from the ignition, slipped out of the car, and started up the hill on foot. Her adrenaline was pumping, her heart was banging, and some rational part of her brain suggested she might want to call the police. Or at least Hank.

She checked her pocket for her cell phone and groaned. At some point during her long marathon of sitting and worrying at the hospital, the battery had run down. It had finally died completely while she'd been back home getting the twins ready for bed, so she'd left it to charge in her kitchen when she returned to the hospital to say good night to Connelly.

Son of a ...

She pulled up short in front of the five-foot-tall fence. The top was just about level with her head. It was decision time: She could still do the smart thing and go back to the car, drive home, and call the authorities.

She gripped the bars and started climbing the fence. She scrabbled to the top and then dropped down lightly to the lawn on the other side, landing in a low crouch. She crept along the property line through the darkness, approaching the cottages from the street side.

When she reached the cottages, she skirted around to the back. No windows within reach. No handy fire escapes to climb. No back door. It looked like there was only one way in. She pressed herself against the side wall and caught her breath.

Now what, brainiac? Are you going to just march up and knock on the front door? Considering the lack of other options, yes, it looked like that was the plan.

She squared her shoulders and headed for the front of the cottage. The curtains in the front windows were drawn, but she could see the faint glow from a lamp inside. She pressed her ear against the door and listened but was unable to make out any sounds.

She raised her fist and rapped on the door. Counted to five in her head then rapped again, louder. After a beat, she called out, "It's me, Dr. All-strom. Open the door."

44.

EO STARED AT THE CEILING. He knew he should be sleeping. He wanted to be sleeping. But he was drifting in a post-operative haze of pain medication. He'd dozed all day. And now he was wide awake at one o'clock in the morning. He was too loopy to read, too tired to watch television. Hank was back home with his kids, having left the agents to guard Duc Nyugen. Annabeth was no doubt hunched over her computer, typing furiously.

He wondered if Sasha might still be awake.

He reached for the phone and dialed her cell phone number.

"Hello? Sasha?" his father-in-law answered immediately in a loud whisper.

"Pat? This is Leo. Sasha's not there?"

"Leo, how are you feeling?"

"At the moment, I'm feeling pretty good. I'm just restless. Couldn't sleep, so I thought I'd give Sasha a call."

"We thought she was still at the hospital. She left her phone here after dinner to charge."

Leo twisted his neck. "She left almost an hour ago." Worry crept into his voice.

"Maybe she stopped to pick up diapers or groceries or something," Pat suggested.

"Maybe." Sasha *did* love doing her grocery shopping in the middle of the night when the stores weren't crowded.

"I'm sure she'll be home any minute. I'll have her call you."

"Thanks."

"You try to get some rest, okay? Val and I will come visit you in the morning."

Leo dropped the phone back on to the cradle and tried to ignore the anxiety that was pricking at him through the morphine.

She's just at Giant Eagle, he told himself.

45.

SASHA SHOOK OUT HER HANDS to keep them loose and relieve some tension while she waited for the door to open. She knew she'd have to be ready to pounce or she risked having the door slammed in her face as soon as he realized she wasn't, in fact, Greta Allstrom.

A moment after she announced herself as Allstrom, she heard the sound of a chair scraping across wood. The lock turned in the door and she readied herself.

The door swung wide open. "What are you doing back--?" the man growled.

She was across the threshold before the goon had completed his sentence. Behind him, she could see Dr. Kayser, strapped to a bed, staring at her in open horror.

"Sasha?" he croaked.

"Silence," the man roared as he slammed the door shut and locked it. He grabbed Sasha's upper arm and locked his meaty hand around it, then dragged her across the room to a small desk and chair. He pushed her into the seat. "Sit."

The man was huffing and snorting like an irritated bull. She half-expected him to paw at the ground.

"Who are you?" he demanded.

"My name is Sasha McCandless-Connelly," she said, affecting an unconcerned, conversational tone despite the fact that she was pretty concerned.

The man looked even larger up close. He had a crooked, boxer's nose that had been broken and set poorly, probably multiple times. The clear outline of a shoulder holster and gun showed through his skin-tight suit jacket. And his mouth was set in a cruel, hard line.

"What are you doing here?"

"I'm Dr. Kayser's attorney. I've been looking for him."

"So you broke into a nursing home in the middle of the night?"

"Well, I found him, didn't I?" she countered.

The man made a noise that was half-growl, half-laugh. "I guess you did. Lucky you. Now you'll get to die with him." His tone of voice was scoffing, dismissive.

Good.

Dr. Kayser squeezed his eyes closed.

She locked eyes with the man. She needed him to underestimate her, to view her as completely non-threatening. She figured she was most of the way there. He had about fifteen inches and two hundred pounds on her. He had a gun. And he had no reason to imagine that she was probably the most accomplished Krav Maga practitioner he'd ever encounter in his life.

"Why do you want to kill Dr. Kayser?" she asked.

"That's none of your business, lawyer lady." He stomped across the room. He moved slowly, lumbering in the way big guys tended to do.

"So, what are you? Some kind of bodybuilder?"

There was *no* way someone this big didn't devote long hours to maintenance. And one thing she knew about gym rats was they loved to talk about their routines. Power lifting, Cross-Fit, spinning. Whatever it was, they would gladly tell you all about it at the slightest hint of interest.

"MMA fighter."

Great. The worst possible answer. Mixed martial arts fighters engaged in full-body combat and combined techniques from multiple disciplines. So this guy probably had some moves from judo, Brazilian jui-jitsu, Muay Thai, boxing, and who knew what else.

She was about to concede to herself that this escapade had been one of her poorer decisions. Then, she smoothed her hand over her hair and had to hide a smile.

"So why is a big guy like you picking on a harmless, geriatric doctor?"

He narrowed his eyes. "I already told you, we're not going to chit chat. Just sit there and shut up. When Dr. Allstrom gets back with her supplies, I'll let you watch her slice up your client's brain before I kill you. How's that sound?"

She glanced at Dr. Kayser, who had reopened his eyes and was staring at her bleakly. "I'm so sorry I involved you in this, Sasha."

"They're going to kill you so they can harvest your brain? That's Allstrom's plan? How can she possibly think she'll get away with this?"

"She's desperate. She's mixed up with some bad people, I think. The Alpha Fund. He works for—"

Dr. Kayser stopped mid-sentence and shrank back against the mattress as the man crossed the room with his arm raised. He backhanded Dr. Kayser, and Sasha winced.

"Hey, big guy," she called. "I need to pee. Is that okay?" She stood up and pointed toward the bathroom door, which was ajar.

The man turned away from Dr. Kayser and stared at her, considering the request.

She blinked back at him, trying to project an air of harmlessness.

"Go ahead. Make it quick."

"Thank you."

She scurried across the room to the bathroom. She flipped on the overhead light and then shut and locked the door. She scanned the room quickly, taking an inventory. Lots of grab bars and non-slip mats. Nothing that looked useful for taking down a giant. She pulled open the medicine cabinet. Empty. She flushed the toilet then turned on the water in the sink full blast. She reached up with her left hand and removed the *kanzashi* from the knot on the back of her head and shook out her hair.

Go time. He had size on his side; she needed surprise on hers.

As she started toward the door she glanced at the grab bar near the shower. Above it a white box was set into the wall. A white cord hung from the box with a weight ball on the end.

Could it be? It had to be. This was a discreet version of the emergency pull cord her dad had installed in Nana Alexandrov's bathroom. Hers had a blazing red panel that read "pull cord in case of emergency." But, of course, Golden Village would be more refined about the need to call for help if a resident fell in the bathroom. Could the goon really have forgotten it was in here?

Not her problem. She yanked the cord and headed for the door.

She *hoped* the alarm would only sound in the main building, but apparently, refinement and pretense went out the window when a resident was lying on the bathroom floor. As she pulled open the door, a repetitive *bloop* blared from hidden speakers at full volume, echoing off the tile walls. A bright light blinked overhead. A pissed off, red-faced man loomed in her path.

"What the hell did you do?" he shouted.

She'd never reach his eyes. He was way too tall. But his vulnerable throat was within reach. She lunged forward with the hairpin and jabbed it straight into his throat, piercing his trachea with the point and yanking it straight back out.

He folded forward, wheezing, shaking droplets of blood everywhere. She released the hairpin and landed a fast, solid knife chop to his throat with the outside ridge of her hand. *Add insult to injury.*

His breath came fast and shallow. He went down on his knees. The alarm blared. The light flashed. She burst forward, taking a step with her left foot, and raised her right foot to finish him off with an advancing front kick to the face. As she raised her shin, he reached out with his right hand and grabbed her ankle.

He yanked downward and used her own momentum to pull her to the ground.

Not good. Krav Maga taught fighters to stay on their feet at all costs. Nothing was worse than being on the ground. But MMA fighters grappled on the ground routinely.

Don't panic. Just don't let him mount you.

Given his size, if she let him pin her down, it was over.

She fell to her back and raised her hips in an awkward bridge pose. He still had her right ankle in his hand, so she rolled to the right and kicked wildly with the bottom of her left foot. Her form was bad. Her moves lacked power. But she had to avoid being mounted. She wriggled in an unpredictable pattern from side to side like a fish that had just been landed.

He dropped her foot and lunged forward, kneeling over her, and telegraphing a chokehold. His hands were coming straight at her neck.

She bucked hard to her left and brought her right elbow up and around connecting with his hands, and knocking them to the side. She rolled up, rotated her body, and aimed a left-handed palm strike at his already-damaged throat. She immediately followed with a second strike from the right and then staggered to her feet.

He emitted a high-pitched, wheezy sound like a leaky balloon. She smiled. That was the unmistakable sound of stridor. His airway was collapsing. She was about to take another shot just for good measure, when the sound of furious pounding at the front door penetrated the chaos. The cavalry had arrived.

46.

Thursday afternoon

ASHA SMILED DOWN AT CONNELLY, who was propped up in his hospital bed, cradling a baby in the crook of each arm.

"I miss you guys," he crooned to the twins.

"Good news. You're apparently in such good shape that Dr. Bryant says you can leave tomorrow."

She found it hard to believe that a person could have seventy-five percent of his liver removed and walk out of the hospital two days later. But if anyone could do it, it was Connelly.

He grinned. "I can't wait." Then the smile faded. "How's *he?*"

"They're moving him from the transplant intensive care unit to a bed on the other transplant floor. Usually they try to put related donors close together, but I explained that in this case, the furthest possible room would be preferred." She studied his face. "Unless you want to see him?"

He shook his head. "No. It's over. Speaking of things that are over, how'd Naya's hearing go?"

She cleared her throat. "In light of the, um, circumstances, the judge issued a permanent order shutting down the research study until the university can clear up the whole mess."

'Mess' was perhaps a bit of an understatement. Dr. Kayser had been admitted for observation over his loud protests. Golden Village was being investigated by the commonwealth; Greta Allstrom and her goon, Derrick Harver, were in police custody. The mysterious Alpha Fund had apparently disbanded in the middle of the night—no doubt en route to far-flung destinations that lacked extradition treaties with the United States.

Connelly was staring hard at her. "At some point, you know, we will need to talk about these so-called circumstances."

"Is this going to be some sort of don't forget to take your cell phone when you're breaking into an assisted living facility lecture?"

He closed his eyes briefly and shook his head from side to side. "What am I going to do with you?"

She leaned over the hospital bed. "Tell you what. You just worry about getting out of this joint and we'll call it even."

"Even? How do you figure?"

"Seems as if we each endured some measure of risk to save a life. I know *I'm* so proud of *you*." She blinked innocently at her husband, who had been temporarily rendered speechless.

Check. And mate.

ABOUT THE AUTHOR

Melissa F. Miller is a *USA TODAY* bestselling author and a former commercial litigator. She has practiced in the offices of international law firms in Pittsburgh, PA and Washington, D.C. and in a two-person firm in South Central Pennsylvania. Today she writes full time. When not out on an adventure with her three young children and husband, she's hard at work on her next book. Like Sasha McCandless, she drinks entirely too much coffee; unlike Sasha, she cannot kill you with her bare hands.

CPSIA information can be obtained at www.ICGtesting.com
Printed in the USA
LVOW11s0200070116

469485LV00007B/782/P

9 781940 759128